D0933883

INDIAN ANNIE:

KIOWA CAPTIVE

ALICE MARRIOTT

DAVID McKAY COMPANY, INC.

NEW YORK

INDIAN ANNIE: KIOWA CAPTIVE

COPYRIGHT © 1965 BY

ALICE MARRIOTT

PUBLISHED SIMULTANEOUSLY IN THE DOMINION OF CANADA

First Edition April 1965
Reprinted August 1966

LIBRARY OF CONGRESS CATALOG CARD NUMBER: 65-14134

MANUFACTURED IN THE UNITED STATES OF AMERICA

For
GINNY
who has gone with me

Contents

INDIAN ANNIE:

KIOWA

CAPTIVE

Author's Note

This story is based on actual events and people. Their names have been changed, and a few events have been telescoped, but the factual basis remains.

In the autumn of 1934, with a graduate fellowship from the department of Anthropology, University of Oklahoma, I first visited the Kiowa Indians, in south-western Oklahoma. My object was to compile as complete a picture as I could of Kiowa life in the middle of the last century. At that time people were alive who had lived that life, and who could remember it.

Friendships that began with that first field work have lasted till today. A particularly durable affection is mine for Lillian Goombi (Mrs. George) Hunt. Mrs. Hunt's mother, Millie Durgan Goombi, was a white captive who grew up as a Kiowa and who married a Kiowa.

This is not the story of Millie Durgan, who was captured when she was a small child. This book is put together from the recollections of many people, relatives and descendants of other captives. Eyewitness accounts of many of these incidents found their way into my field notebooks. For others, I recorded secondhand narratives.

I have leaned heavily on *A Quaker among the Indians,* by Thomas Battey, an account of Kiowa life at the time of the tribe's capitulation to the white man. Battey was an intelligent man, a keen observer, and possessed of a feeling heart. If at times he wished that God had called him to some other field, still he put up with the "whim-sicalities" of those of God's red children among whom his lot had fallen. Battey was scrupulously fair and unfailingly kind in his observations and comments on Kiowa character and ways.

In other books I have tried to show the life of the rebellious Kiowas who resisted the changes white men brought in their lives. In this one I have tried to show what happened to those Kiowas who took the peace road, and tried to adjust to the new ways that were introduced to them.

To all the many people who have helped me—too many to list; too many even to count—my warmest and most humble gratitude.

Alice Marriott
Oklahoma City
April, 1965

Chapter One

Gone to Texas

The sun rose over the edge of the earth, red and angry-looking, like a boil. Already, before six in the morning, you knew how hot the day was going to be. All around the sod house the flat lands spread, as far as the blue fence of sky which shut in the earth. There were no trees, no clear brown water boiling along the creek beds and down the hillsides—no hills, to break the flatness of this world. Texas was a place where you could see whatever there was to see. The trouble was, there was nothing to look at.

Annie picked up the milk pail and plodded through the yellow dust to the house. If you got your chores done early, before the real heat of the day closed down on the plains, then you could rest in the shade at the side of the house at the nooning. Father sometimes said he thought the children could stay out in the fields all day, but Mother wouldn't allow the girls to work in the heat.

"No, Paw," she always said. "Redheads they are and beauties they are not, and our girls'll never be rich, but at least they're not going to be farm hands. Two hours

each, morning and evening, I will permit, but that's all."
Mother had been a schoolteacher, and she talked like one.

Now Annie pushed back the tow-sack curtain hanging at the door, and entered the one room that was the whole inside of the sod house. Mother had the room all laid out, like their old house back in Tennessee. The kitchen was in one corner and the table in another. The beds were at the back of the room, separated by burlap curtains like the one hung over the door. Father had built a real fireplace for them, instead of getting by with a mud hearth under a hole in the roof. They all took turns watering down the dirt floor, and keeping it swept smooth and clean.

There was a separate soddie for James and Sadie and Deuteronomy, their freedmen. Back in Tennessee, before all the trouble started, James and Sadie and their little boy had been the Donovan family's slaves. After they all got out and went to Texas, Father frequently reminded the children that the Negroes weren't slaves any more. They were freedmen, and if they had stayed on in Tennessee James would have had the right to vote, as Father did. But out here on the Texas flats there didn't seem to be any elections, so James' freedom didn't make such a difference.

This was all such a changed world from the one Annie Donovan had been used to! She could clearly remember the comfortable old log house in the Cumberland Valley, with its walls whitewashed inside and out each spring. Even the house was not as clear to her memory, though, as the shape of the hills rising behind it and the valley opening out in front. The cornfields were planted in terraces on the hillsides, and the cows were pastured along the stream that flowed through the valley. There was a garden behind the house, Annie remembered, with carrots and turnips and mint and sage all mixed in with the okra-gumbo and pepper plants that Sadie raised. There were a clothesline and an ash hopper, and a table and benches were set out under the old walnut tree for summer suppers. The house itself was a hog-trot house. From the garden end of the passage you could see clear through, and on out to the road.

Annie was standing there, looking through at the road, when the blue troops came riding into the picture framed for her by the hog-trot. The soldiers stopped in front of the house, and the officer—the man with boards on his shoulders—took off his hat and bowed to Mother as politely as if he'd been Southern-born, for all he was a Yankee. He'd asked permission for his men to drink from the well, and Mother had given it. Afterward she said that as much as she hated the sight of a Yankee, she couldn't let the horses suffer.

When the men had drunk their fill, and the horses had watered at the hollowed-out log trough, the officer took off his cap, and bowed to Mother again.

"Thank you, ma'am," he said. "I take it kindly that you'd give us water. There's a-many that won't. Maybe you haven't heard the news? General Lee surrendered yesterday to General Grant, at Appomatox Court House. The war's over, and thank God for that."

"Yes, thank God for that," Mother whispered, her eyes fixed on the Yankee officer's face and the tears flowing from them, right down her cheeks, like two creeks on a hillside. "Thank God for that, at least."

"Ma'am," said the Yankee officer, "if I'd a-knowed you'd take it that way, I swear to God I'd a-told you different. I swear it, ma'am."

Mother stood there with her head up and the tears drying on her cheeks, proud as a banty rooster. "What troops are you?" she asked.

"Fourth Indiana, ma'am."

"Well, you're on your way home," Mother said. "Ride on. Go back to Indiana, and leave us to put our lives together again when once you're gone. You've left us precious little to do it with."

"Yes, ma'am," the officer said. He swung up in his saddle. "I hope your men get back safe and well."

Looking down at Mother, he touched a finger to the peak of his cap. Then he flung up his arm, and shouted, "Forward-Hooooh!" and the big horses padded away along the road.

Annie was eight years old that very day. She didn't

[6]

understand everything that Mother and the officer had said, but she never forgot a word of it. Later in the day she asked Mother what it all meant.

"Thank God, it means that your father and Bud are coming home," Mother answered, "and that they're both alive and we have a roof over our heads. But the War Between the States is over and the Confederacy is defeated. We can't tell what in the world will happen to any of us next." She put out her arms, and gathered Annie in, and held her tight. "We've been lucky," Mother said, with her lips moving against Annie's hair. "We've kept our house and our farm, and some of the stock. The fighting hasn't come close to us. We have the cows and chickens, and we have the garden, and we've never starved. Other people are a lot worse off, poor things."

Father and Bud came home a month later. Annie saw them first framed through the hog-trot, coming along the road. Only they were riding mules, not horses. They'd left home on good saddle horses, and here they came back riding plow mules. Annie laughed and laughed. She didn't know for sure if she were laughing at the mules or for joy that Father and Bud were home.

They had a fine dinner that night: possum James had trapped, and sweet potatoes and gravy, and pecan pie, served in the big room on the west side of the hog-trot. Then the children went to bed with the doors to the passage open, so they could see the grown-ups sitting out in the hog-trot in the moonlight, talking and talking.

In the morning, after prayers, and Grace and breakfast, Father told them right flat out that they were moving.

"With a Yankee government running things, times are going to be hard," he said. "Lots of men in our outfit are talking about going to Texas. Down there, a man can anyhow run his own farm his own way. We'll sell out for what we can get, and go West. Maybe we'll even go as far as California."

After the auction was over, they were down to the clothes they stood up in, the two milk cows, a crate of chickens, one sow and a barrow, and the things Mother said she just had to have to keep house. Father had kept both mules and the four farm horses. He spent what he said was a lot of money for a big farm wagon with a brown canvas top.

The night before they were going to leave, with everything all packed and loaded in the wagon, James came and stood at the back door, scraping the side of his foot against the doorsill.

"Cap'n," he asked, "what's going to happen to me and Sadie and the boy?"

"Why, whatever you like, Jim," Father said. "You're

free now. The government's set you free. You can go wherever you like and do whatever you want to do."

"Can we, Cap'n?" James asked. "Is that for sure, sir?"

"It's for sure," Father declared.

"Then we'd like to go with you and Miss Mary, Cap'n, sir," said James. "You're the only close folks we have. We'd like to go to Texas along with the rest of the family, sir."

"I can't pay you if you go, Jim. All the money I had in the world was in Confederate banks, and it's gone. We haven't got much more than will feed and travel us. You're a good hand. Folks will need help. You could get plenty of work around here."

"If you got enough to feed and travel us, Cap'n, all right. If not, we'll manage to tag along some way. I can keep us all in meat, trapping squirrels and possums. We can stop at any stream we come to, and get some cat and maybe perch. They're all good eating. I can keep supplies coming along."

"Thank you, Jim. We might do better with you than without you, and we sure would miss you if you stayed behind."

"And another thing, Cap'n. Sadie can't let go of Miss Mary, or Annie and Katherine. She's got to be with them, and with Bud and Danny, the same as she's got to be with me and Deut. They're our folks."

So when they left Tennessee, they all left together. Before he climbed in the wagon, Bud took a charred stick, and wrote on the closed front door the letters G.T.T.

"What does that mean?" Annie inquired.

"Gone to Texas." Bud grinned. "You wait, you'll see it on other places."

They saw the letters G.T.T. many times as they went west. It was both sad and defiant; sad because it was the signature to the final surrender of the Confederacy, Mother said, and defiant, because people wouldn't stay and be put upon while they could still get out, Father declared.

Two years and one day later, on the morning after her tenth birthday, Annie remembered their leaving, but the trip itself had blurred a little in her mind. They went through hilly country all the way through Tennessee, and across the Arkansas slopes, and down through the Indian Nations. Everywhere the country looked bare and untended. All the men had been away to war, and some of them would never come back. The women were worn out with the effort of living, without more than trying to keep things together.

She remembered one evening. They were down in the Choctaw Nation, and just before crossing the Red River into Texas. Father stopped the mules and they made camp for the night near a backwoodsy-looking farm. It looked just like any other farm in that part of the world to Annie. The woman who was pounding corn in a log mortar in the dooryard wore a sprigged-calico dress like Mother's sprigged-calico dresses. She was a young woman, pounding with strong arms. Her straight black braid swung to and fro on her back as she pounded, like the pendulum of the old clock they had given the preacher before they left home.

"Go and ask her if we can trade for some corn meal," Mother instructed Annie.

Annie skipped off. It was getting on for fall now, and Mother made her wear shoes, which were heavy and got in her way, but they still didn't stop her from skipping. A pack of yellow dogs came boiling around the corner of the house, but dropped to their bellies as soon as the woman spoke to them.

The woman looked at Annie and smiled, a white smile in a brown face. Then she raised her arm, and pushed back the soft loose strands of hair that had fallen onto her forehead with her wrist. She spoke to Annie.

From the way the woman's voice rose at the end of the sentence, Annie knew she must have asked a question, but Annie didn't understand a word the woman said.

"Mother wants to trade you something for some corn meal." Annie spoke very slowly and distinctly.

The woman shook her head. She looked as puzzled as

Annie felt. They stood and smiled at each other helplessly. Finally Annie pointed with her finger—she knew
Mother would never forgive her for being so rude, if she
found out—at the mortar. The woman reached over, took
a handful of meal, and let it run through her fingers. She
raised her eyebrows—eyebrows so fine that Annie could
barely see that they arched across her face. Annie nodded.

From just inside the house door, the woman brought
a basket, made from flat cane splints, and filled it with
the meal. She held out the basket for Annie to take. After
a moment, Annie took it. She had no idea how to ask the
woman what she wanted in exchange.

Back at the wagon, Mother looked at the meal. "How
much did the lady want for it?" she queried.

Annie looked at her helplessly. "I don't know," she
replied.

"You don't know!" Mother exclaimed. "A big girl
like you! Why didn't you ask her?"

"I did, but I couldn't understand what she said."

"Nonsense!" said Mother. "You go straight back and
ask her again, Annie Donovan. The idea, taking something without paying for it! And from a stranger, too!"

Annie dutifully went back. Again she and the woman
spoke to each other, and again neither of them understood
a word the other said. Finally Annie held out her hand.
The woman took it, and let Annie lead her to the wagon.

Father and Jim had just come in from hunting, carry-

ing a small white-tailed deer slung on a pole between
them. They set the deer down on the ground, and Mother
and Annie explained their problem. The brown woman
stood quietly while they all talked together.

Finally Father looked at the woman again, more carefully. Then he smiled, and she smiled her white friendly
smile back at him.

"I'll just bet she's an Indian," Father said. "We had
Cherokee troops with us at Pea Ridge— good men, too.
She looks Indian to me." He turned to the woman.
"Cherokee?" he asked.

The woman caught the word quickly, and shook her
head.

"Chahtah," she said, pointing to herself. "Chahtah."

"Chahtah?" Father repeated.

"Chahtah." The woman nodded her head.

"She must mean Choctaw," Father observed.

Again the woman nodded, and said, "Chahtah."

"Well," Mother remarked, "I never thought the day
would come when I'd be buying meal off a real live
Indian!" She studied the woman. "Looks about like
anybody else, it seems to me. You'd never know
what she was unless you heard her speak. Well, Paw, you
do so well talking to her, ask her what she wants for the
meal."

Father gestured toward the deer on the ground, and
made a motion as if he were cutting. The Choctaw

[13]

woman nodded. Father got his long knife, and skinned out a hindquarter for her. She shook her head, pointing to the meal basket.

"Does she want more?" Mother demanded. "Seems to me that's an awful lot of meat for not more than a pound of corn meal."

"I don't know," Father replied. He took up the knife and gestured toward the deer. The woman shook her head. Suddenly she turned and ran back to her house, her bare feet patting the ground, and her full skirts swinging around them. She disappeared inside. A moment later she was running back to their camp again, with a heavy-looking tow-sack in her hand.

The Indian woman set the sack on the ground, knelt beside it, and opened it. The bag was full of cracked corn, ready to be pounded into fine meal, or cooked as it was. Their new friend gathered the neck of the sack together again, tied it, and then held the bag out to Mother.

"Why, thank you!" Mother exclaimed. "That's a lot of corn for a little bit of meat!"

The Donovan family stayed near the Choctaw farm five days, resting the team, washing their clothes in the spring, and getting acquainted with the Indian woman. Her husband was away, but she did not seem to be afraid to stay alone. Probably that was because of the way the big yellow dogs roamed and guarded the place. Chahtah penned them up in the morning, so they wouldn't hurt anyone she knew. At night the dogs went free, to guard. Annie could hear them sometimes as she dropped to sleep in the wagon, hunting through the woods and belling as they hunted.

On the fifth evening they heard cattle lowing, and men shouting at the beasts. Up the trail from the south a dust cloud rolled toward them. Presently the shapes of the trail herd and its drivers formed through the mistiness, and then became real. Chahtah came running out of her house, and stood in the dooryard, waiting. A young man rode out of the group that guided the herd, dismounted before her, and laid his cheek against hers for a moment. They went inside the house together. The other drivers took the herd on, to pasture for the night below the spring.

Later Chahtah and the young man came to visit the Donovan camp. The man could speak and understand a little English.

Somehow, he and Father made out together. His English name was Bill Jim, he said, but his wife had no English name. He called her Te-Ata, and when he said the name he pointed up to the eastern sky, as if he were pointing out a star.

Bill Jim said he had been down to Texas to buy cattle. He would feed and fatten them here in the Choctaw Nation, and then drive them northwest, to Fort Sill, to sell to the soldiers there.

"Soldiers bad mens," Bill Jim remarked. "Shoot, shoot Injuns. Push um along down the road." He smiled brightly, like his wife. "Soldiers' money good," he went on. "Buy, buy piece goods for ole laty, boots for ole man, brass kettle, knife—buy, buy, buy."

Annie wondered what he meant. She had listened to her grandfathers' tales of Indians in Kentucky in the early days, and of how that piece of Dark and Bloody Ground got its name from the way the Indians had massacred the whites. As well as Annie knew, it had never entered anybody's head that maybe the Indians felt massacred, too. But Bill Jim certainly seemed to think so. He did not hold it against the Donovan family personally, though. Before they left the next morning, Bill Jim gave Father all the advice he could about roads and water and the best route to go.

That was how they had come to be on these flat lands west of the Brazos River—west even of the Trinity. Bill Jim said there was open range country there, and that Father could raise cattle. The country was certainly open and the cattle ranged widely, Father agreed when they had lived in west Texas a year, but raising stock was a different matter from what it had been at home.

"Those damned Indians!" Father raged, when one of his best brood cows lay dead under the baking sun, with only her ribs and tongue cut out.

"Choctaws, Paw?" Danny asked. After all, they were the only Indians the children knew about firsthand.

[16]

"Comanches, more likely," Father answered. "Maybe even Kiowas. They come down from the north and shoot the cattle as if they thought they were buffalo. Look at the waste! Most of the carcass left lying there to rot!"

"Well, the meat hasn't rotted yet," Mother reminded him. "The least we can do is save some of it. Get busy, you and Bud. You can skin it out right here. We'll butcher and dry the meat Indian fashion."

The Donovans had learned a lot in that first year. They had learned to dry meat in the sun; to haul every drop of water that they used from the creek two miles away; to burn cow chips for fuel because there was no wood, and to live in the sod house winter and summer.

Their nearest neighbors were five miles away as the crow flies, and farther than that by the wagon ruts that wound and dipped, in and out of dry creek beds and across the prairies. There was no school, but Mother gave the young ones lessons every day, and kept them up with their reading and writing and figuring.

Father taught them only one formal lesson, but he taught it in so many words. "If the Indians ever come near us," he told them over and over, "don't try to run or hide. They can catch up with you wherever you are, if you're out in the open. Cut back to the house, or, if that's too far away, cut off across the flats to the Hurley's, or go to the Cantrells' house. Get behind walls as quickly as you can—and stay there."

"What would the Indians do if they came, Paw?" Danny asked. Danny was at the age when he was always asking questions.

"The least they would do is to slaughter the stock and run off the horses," Father replied. "The worst would be to kill all of us, or steal one of you. Don't take any chances. Cut for a house as fast as you can, if you see them coming."

It sounded exciting and dangerous to Annie, part of the thrill of coming west to Texas. The most wonderful thing that could have happened to her back home was getting lost in the woods. Annie knew that was a safe excitement; if she sat still and waited, James or Bud or Father would find her.

What kind of excitements did Indian children have, Annie wondered. Would you like riding and living in a tent if you did it every day? There *had* to be Indian children; the dangerous wild Indians her father was talking about must have grown up to be fierce and strong. But nobody ever mentioned the Indian women and children; nobody ever saw them. Annie wondered where the mothers and their children were and what they did. She did not wonder out loud, however. Somehow, she had a feeling Father would scold her and Bud would laugh at her.

As a matter of fact, the trouble with these Indians was that nobody ever saw any of them. Te-Ata and her husband had had nothing to hide. They moved around openly like all the people Annie had ever known. She remembered that you could watch them, or go to their house to visit, as much as you liked. But the Kiowas and Comanches! They were here today and gone tomorrow, as Father said. When they went something always went with them: cattle, the mare and her new foal Father had given Annie, or maybe just corn from the fields. There was always something missing.

"Red thieves!" Father stormed, when they found that the mare and her colt were gone.

Annie sat down on the doorsill and cried. Little as he was, Danny put his arm around her and comforted her.

"Don't cry, Sister," he said. "When I grow up I'm going to chase those Indians. I'll make them give Buttercup back to you!"

"I hate them!" Annie wept. "I hate them even worse than Yankees! I'll always hate them! I wish I was a man, so I could go after them and kill them."

"Don't cry, honey," Mother soothed her," and don't hate anybody—not even Yankees—if you can help it. About all we've got between us and the Kiowas is the soldiers at Fort Sill, Union troops or no Union troops."

"We'd better head there. if we ever really need help," Father said.

"Let's just pray we never do," said Mother quietly. And so far they hadn't needed such help, thought ten-year-old Annie Donovan, pouring the milk from the bucket into the rising pans. And both the Jersey cows were in milk; the chickens were coming along—those the hawks hadn't taken—and maybe they would make out living in Texas, after all.

Chapter Two

Summer Sunday

Sundays were different in Texas. Back home they all went to church every Sunday of the world. Here there was no church to attend. Once a month the Presbyterian minister came around, riding from Fort Sill to Fort Worth, and on west from there, as far as he could find any settlements to visit. In good weather, his wife rode with him.

The Donovan family was up even before the summer daylight edged the earth, on First Sundays of the month. After all, they were farmers. Cows and chickens don't know a thing about the days of the week. Feeding, watering, milking, and egg-gathering chores go on at a farm on Sundays, just as they do any other day.

The difference was that on First Sundays the chores had to be done earlier in the morning than usual, so the family could get a good early start for services. They had to go ten miles across country to the Cantrells' house, where the minister stayed and services were held. Mother and Annie packed a basket lunch, and all the other women did the same. After Morning Prayer, they all shared their food with one another.

The Cantrells were quality. They had come out from Virginia, which they always pronounced as if it were spelled with an "F" instead of with a "V." Mrs. Cantrell still had the silverware and fine Chelsea china her house-man had hidden from the Yankees. After the blue coats were gone, as she told her guests once each month, the Negro man had dug everything out of the manure pile, and returned every single bit of it to her intact. Some guests, hearing this story on their first First Sunday, neglected to eat afterward. But in time, as Annie had learned, you can get used to anything.

She helped her mother dress Katherine, while Bud and Father and Danny scrubbed themselves in a washtub, just outside the door. Katherine was always excited, and today she twisted and turned, wiggled and pouted, worse than usual.

"Hold still!" Annie ordered, exasperated. "I can't ever button you up, if you wiggle like that. You're worse than a Kiowa."

"I am not!" Katherine flared. "Maw! You make her quit, now! She's calling me names!"

"What did you call her, Annie?" Mother asked around the end of a braid. She was holding it in her teeth while she plaited the hair on the other side of her head.

"Nothing," Annie said, "I didn't call her any name. I told her to hold still, that's all."

"She did too, Maw," Katherine insisted. "She called me an awful name. She said I was—"

[22]

"I don't want to hear it," Mother declared, once her mouth was free of the braid. "I don't like tattletales any better than I do name-callers. Hurry up, now, both of you. Your father's ready with the team; I can hear them."

The horses were stamping and jerking their heads in protest against the flies. Bud and Danny, James and Sadie and Deut, were already seated on quilts in the wagon box. Bud got down, to hand Mother up over the wheel to her place on the seat beside Father; then he helped both girls get in. Last of all, he jumped back in the wagon box, and shot home the bolts that held the tailboard.

Annie sat carefully. Her best dress was made with hoops cut down from one of Mother's old ones, and sitting was a problem at best. If she sat on the back of her skirt, the hoops tilted up front and showed her pantalettes. They were nice white muslin pantalettes, with lace edging the ruffles, but Annie knew she was too old to show them, except accidentally. On the other hand, if she pulled up the back of her skirt and sat on the seat of her pantalettes, with the hoop free in front, she showed off her petticoats. The best way was to scrouch down inside the hoops, and hope that no high wind would come along, to catch and tilt her skirt, in spite of her efforts to be modest.

The sun shone and the wind blew. The wind always blew in this part of Texas. It ran along the ground like a hunting dog, worrying the grass clumps as it looked for rabbits, tossing the treetops as it hunted wild turkeys, pulling at your hair and playing with it roughly. Even a sunbonnet was little protection against the Texas wind; little puffs pried inside its scuttle and tickled your forehead with any stray locks they could find.

The prairie world spread all around them. Annie remembered her *McGuffey's Eclectic Fifth Reader,* and the picture of a boat on a calmed ocean on one page. The ocean went on for miles around the dot that was the boat. And the prairies did the same thing; they surrounded the dot that was the wagon, and moved with it, endlessly changing and endlessly the same. If it hadn't been for the creek and the crossing, Annie thought to herself, you could hardly tell that you were moving.

She looked at Bud, and thought how handsome her big brother was. His hair was as dark as his eyes, and his skin was tanned by the sun to the color of Mother's mahogany table. He had his hat on his head, and Annie could tell by the way it was set in place that he had his hair plastered down with water underneath.

"You got your hair slicked, Bud?" she asked innocently.

Bud turned red under his tan, and didn't answer.

Danny said, "He's got it all slicked down. I saw him. He even put bear grease on it."

"That the truth, Mr. Bud?" James inquired.

"Aw . . ." Bud began.

"I know why he's all got up!" Katherine announced. "He's going to see Mary Sue Cantrell, that's why!"

"Is it, Bud? Bud, is that the truth? Did you get all fussed up to go see Mary Sue Cantrell, Bud? Is that it?" Danny began to pester.

"Aw . . ." said Bud again.

"You just know that's it," Sadie remarked sedately. "When a young man's ready to go courtin', that's how he starts, slickin' down his hair. After that he has to have a clean ironed shirt every day—"

"You shut up!" Bud shouted. "You quit, Sadie! It's bad enough having the little ones picking on me—"

"That'll do," Father said from the wagon seat, never turning his head. "That's enough of that. If Bud wants pomade and a clean ironed shirt, that's his business. The rest of you leave him alone. It's no way to act on the way to worship, anyway. Let me hear you all say your catechisms, now, and not another word."

They were still busy quizzing each other about the *Westminster Shorter Catechism* when they drove into the Cantrells' yard. Bud dropped the tailgate and scrambled out to help Mother get down. Father lifted Katherine out of the wagon bed. Then he turned politely and admired Colonel Cantrell's greyhound, holding out his hand so that Annie and Sadie could balance their hoops to the ground. James and Deut led the team away, and hitched them with the other horses in the shade of the chinaberry tree outside the yard fence. Annie wondered, as she always did, how Colonel Cantrell had been able

[25]

to find the one lone chinaberry tree in all west Texas. Everybody else she knew had to make out with mesquite, and that gave about as much shade as yucca.

The men clustered on the porch, but the ladies went inside, and gathered in Mrs. Cantrell's parlor. The Cantrells did not live in a soddie. They had had planks hauled from the railhead, all the way down from Indian Territory, and they lived in a house. It had two rooms and an upstairs loft. The other room was the kitchen. In spite of the four-poster bed in one corner, Mrs. Cantrell called the front room the parlor. After all, the piano stood there.

Katherine went to play under the piano with the other little girls. Annie sat carefully on a chair between her mother and Mary Sue Cantrell. Mary Sue was older, but she was nice. Even if Annie had had girls her own age to play with, she could hardly have gone crawling under the piano with her hoops on. Besides, Annie liked to sit still and listen to the ladies. She couldn't understand everything they said, but it all sounded exciting, and that made things interesting.

"So I told her," said Mrs. McGully, the minister's wife, "I told her, you've got an awful nerve, I said. I told her right out, here I've trusted you, and I thought you were my friend, and you go and steal my potato-salad recipe. Yes, steal, I said. It's no better than thieving to sit there tasting every bite, so's you can remember what's in it."

"It's a shame," Mother agreed.

"Ladies!" called Colonel Cantrell. "Are we all ready? I believe Mr. McGully wants to start the services."

There was a hush throughout the room. Annie heard the minister scrambling down from the loft, where he and his wife had spent the night.

Without being called, the men knew that the time had come. They shuffled through the open door and filled the back of the room. Mrs. Cantrell sat down at the piano, struck a chord, and shook her head because the instrument was out of tune. Everybody began to sing "Abide with me."

It was such a sweet sad tune! And the words were sweet and sad. Annie felt tears she didn't expect and couldn't understand coming into her eyes, and a knot filling up her throat. There was nothing painful about her sadness; in a way she rather enjoyed it, and even enjoyed knowing that she could feel sad, with her family all around her and a summer Sunday outside. She could hear James' voice, deeper than all the other men's voices put together, rolling out, and sustaining them all. She could hear Sadie's voice, light and clear and high, soaring like a meadow lark's. And close beside her Katherine was doing her four-year-old best, humming and stumbling along through the tune like a little honey bee.

At the end of the tune, Mr. McGully spread out his

arms. "Let us pray," he said, and they all bowed their heads.

"Oh, Lord, our God," Mr. McGully began, and that was as far as he went. Sudden, fierce, barking yells broke out around the house. Women screamed. Men who had guns reached for them, and some fired through the windows. A smell of smoke seeped into the room, and grew stronger by the minute.

"My horses!" shouted Colonel Cantrell. At the same moment his wife cried, "Mary Sue! My silverware!"

Annie reached for Katherine and drew her close, feeling for Mother with her other hand.

"It's Kiowas!" Mother cried, and then, as smoke and little flames curled through the open kitchen door, she screamed, "Get outside, children! Run for the creek! We'll all be killed for sure if we stay here!" Annie saw her pick up Danny, as she herself bent to lift Katherine.

Then they were all outside, crowding through the outer door and onto the porch, to escape the flames that had already taken the kitchen. Naked men on horseback were all around them, shouting, firing, waving their arms, and trying to frighten the women and children and split them off from the group of men. Annie saw a man riding right straight at her. Still clinging to Katherine, she turned to run away. The movement undid her. Her treacherous hoops tilted and swayed in the Texas wind and the rush of her motion. It swung up over her face, at the same moment that she tripped on a root of the chinaberry tree and went down. The last thing Annie remembered before she fell into blackness was seeing James pick up Katherine.

Chapter Three

Beginning Again

Annie awakened, knowing she was on the back of a horse, but not knowing how she knew it. Her body ached in a thousand places, and her head was all one large pain. She could feel her arms hanging, heavy and sore, at her sides. The pressure of a rope around her waist bound her to someone who rode behind her.

Painfully, Annie forced her eyes open. Night and its darkness were all around them, with the prairie stars pressed down close over their heads. Annie wanted to reach out and touch a star; if she did that, she was sure, she would be safe. But the stars were too far away for her to touch them, and her arm was too heavy to hold up. She let it drop down at her side again.

Her movement must have told the other person that she was awake, though, for she felt a hard hand squeeze her shoulder, and heard a man's voice grunt a single word. Annie didn't know what word it was, but she was sure that he meant for her to be quiet. And then suddenly she was too weary for anything. Her body drooped forward, supported by the rope, and let itself be claimed again by sleep.

When Annie awoke the next time it was almost daylight. Pink and gold clouds were filling the sky and floating off toward the deep western blue that was all that was left of the night. The horse had stopped. Annie could smell its sweat, and the sweat of the man behind her. She turned her head and looked around cautiously. They were in the midst of a group of men, naked except for their breechclouts and moccasins. Annie had time to wonder where they got the cloth to make the breechclouts before the men kicked their horses forward and they all rode into a canyon.

The canyon was steep-walled and winding, and the horses picked their way along the bottom for several minutes. Then the canyon walls made an almost-right-angled turn, and the group of riders came out on a little green lawn. The bottom of the canyon widened here, and grass grew thickly. A stream ran clean and clear out of one red rock wall and filled a natural stone basin at its foot. The sight of that clear running water made Annie want to cry. It was like the clear creek water back home.

Her captor untied the rope that bound them together, and dropped down from the horse. Annie slid after him, and lay on the ground where she landed, too stiff and weak to get up until the man took hold of her arm and lifted her. The man's touch, in a way, was reassuring;

somehow Annie understood that he was not going to hurt her. She looked at his face.

Sweat had streaked and runnelled the paint the Kiowa had carefully applied to his face before the raid, so that now he looked as if he wore a carved and painted wooden mask. The man's hair hung loose over his left shoulder, and was hacked short above his right ear. The whole rim of the ear was pierced with holes, from which hung lengths of gold and silver chains.

He was a short man, barely a head taller than Annie herself, but his shoulders were wide and his chest was deep, and she knew the long smooth muscles of his arms were very strong, for she had felt their strength. His hands and feet were small—almost as small as a woman's. There was no hair on his naked body, and his face was as clean as Father's when he had just shaved. His dark eyes were puckered from the sun, beneath eyebrows almost as delicate as Te-Ata's. His head and face seemed too large and heavy for the rest of him.

The man looked at Annie for a moment, and then his heavy face cracked into a wide white grin. Annie looked down at herself, wondering what about her was so funny. The frame of her betraying hoop still swung from her waist, but the skirt of her dress was almost gone; torn and shredded by the mesquite bushes that must have clutched and clung to it during the night ride. From the waist down she had nothing on but petticoats and pantalettes. Above her waist her dress was less torn, but she could feel the morning's coolness sweep through a great tear between her shoulders.

Now the man spoke, to Annie's surprise, in English. The speech was hard for him; he shaped his words one at a time, with much effort. "Who? You?" he asked.

Annie stared at him before she answered. "Annie Donovan," she finally brought out.

The Kiowa shook his head thoughtfully. He turned, and called something to the men who had clustered about the spring, and were drinking from it. One of the older men detached himself from the group and came across to them. Annie's captor waited until the other reached them; then he repeated his question.

"Who? You?"

Annie felt sure she was going to cry. She fought against the tears. Her head ached, so suddenly and sharply that she cried out and put her hand up to it. "Annie Donovan. I'm Annie Donovan," she reiterated numbly.

The second man reached out and drew the hand away from her forehead. His own hands touched her head, here and there, lightly. He spoke to the first man. Annie could not understand a word of the garble that they spit out at each other. She was too tired to listen; too tired to think. Her legs gave way under her again, and she sank down on the grass.

Both men squatted beside her. "You? Sick?" her captor inquired.

Annie lay and looked at him. "My head pains me,"

she said, and then the tears came pouring down her cheeks.

The men waited to speak again until she quieted; waited without punishing or scolding her, and without comforting her. That surprised Annie; everything and everybody around her surprised her, but nothing was surprising in itself. She looked at the men, and suddenly the smoke, the shouts, and the gunfire in the Cantrells' living room swept back across her mind. She shrank away from the men, and realized they had noticed her movement and her quick fright. Then Annie thought of Father. He was a Captain in the Confederate Army. He wouldn't want her to show that she was scared—not ever. She pointed her finger directly at the man who had taken her prisoner.

"Who? You?" she parroted his question.

The man took hold of her finger and turned it away from himself and in the direction of the canyon wall. He did not like to be pointed at, that was clear. Annie asked again,

"Who? You?"

This time the man answered her. "Sahnko," he said. He jerked his chin at the other man. "Dohawsan. We. Kiowas."

So they both had names, although they were Indians. That was some comfort. And anyway Annie was too tired and sore to be afraid for long. She only hoped they

[34]

would not hurt her and she would not disgrace her raising by crying any more. Sahnko spoke again.

"I take you," he said, still spacing his words wide apart. "Had . . ." he hesitated, "li'l girl." Then he said in a rush of blurring syllables, "Li'l girl. She go dead. I take you."

He wasn't going to hurt her, Annie thought, surprised. She was still afraid of him, but at least he was human. He had had a little girl, and he missed her and grieved for her. He wanted another little girl to take her place.

"You drink. Eat," Sahnko instructed her. "Sleep. To-night go." He helped Annie up, and led her across the floor of the canyon to the spring.

Annie drank as Sahnko did, from her cupped hands. Then he opened a buckskin sack that hung around his neck, and poured out a small handful of yellow meal.

Annie imitated Sahnko, putting a small pinch of the meal in her mouth at a time, and washing each pinch down with a sip of water. The meal had no taste, but it was filling. She felt stronger and better, and her head did not ache so much.

After they had eaten, Annie lay down on the ground and dropped into a dead, dreamless sleep. She wakened, to feel Sahnko shaking her. The bottom of the canyon was in deep shadow, but there was still light and color in the sky above the rim. Men and horses were moving

[35]

about in the shadows, drinking again, eating pinches of yellow meal, preparing to move on. Annie's head still ached dully, but her body was not as sore as it had been in the morning.

Sahnko lifted Annie back on the horse, swung himself up behind her, and tied his rawhide rope around them both. The group of riders wound up out of the canyon and onto the open prairie again.

Afterward, the whole ride blurred over in Annie's memory. She had never in her life felt as she did then, and she never wanted to again. She was afraid to think—afraid to remember. Questions piled up behind her aching forehead, and it hurt worse from their pressure.

Mother and Father. Bud and Danny. James and Sadie and Deut. And Katherine—her little sister—Katherine? Had they all got away? Were they living or dead? If the rest of her family had been captured, someone else must have taken them. They were not with these Kiowas; Annie herself was their only prisoner.

Maybe other Indians had taken part in the attack on the Cantrell farm. Perhaps Katherine and Danny had been carried away to somewhere else. Annie straightened her body, and sat stiff in front of Sahnko. Sure as she lived, some day she'd find the others, wherever they were. If they were alive. Her muscles went slack again. But she had to find her own people, and she would. She would look for them wherever she went, for as long as she lived.

They rode for three more nights, and Annie fought her thoughts and memories every foot of the way. She wondered about Sahnko. He was kind to her, in his way. He picked her up and tied her to him on the horse's back, but he never hurt her. He didn't tie her up when they stopped to rest and eat, but encouraged her to move around and stretch. He seemed sure that Annie wouldn't run away.

Well, for that matter, she wouldn't. There was nowhere for her to run. Part of the bitter ache choking Annie's throat was that she couldn't—needn't—run. There was nowhere to go and she knew it.

Dawn was whitewashing the sky of the fourth morning. Annie had seen the shapes of hills, cloud-like, to the north, when they started out the previous evening. Now the hills were close at hand. Not high hills like the Tennessee mountains; rather, rounded and bare, scattered with gray boulders. Scrubby low twisty cedars grew amongst the rocks.

She saw a cluster of brown-and-white cone-shaped tents at the foot of the rise. There were dome-shaped brush-covered shelters set among the tents, looking cool and refreshing even from this distance.

In among the tents and the arbors there were pole racks, like clotheslines without ropes, and black tattered rags hung from them. As they came closer, Annie could see that behind some camps there were other racks, or tripods, and that shields, weapons, and variously shaped bundles were carefully hung from these.

Horses grazed in an open meadow, near the camp but away from it, beside a little stream. The horses were watched by three or four boys, some of them younger than Danny.

Before Annie had time to get her bearings, the dogs came flinging themselves out of the tents and surged up on the horses. Sahnko struck at them with his quirt, not as if he really meant to hurt them, but only to chase them away. It seemed as if everyone in the village came out of the tents at the same moment; chasing the dogs, calling and laughing with excitement, and throwing their arms around the riders as, one by one, the men dismounted.

Sahnko went on through the main camp, and stopped before one of the smaller tents. He sat still for a moment, smiling at the woman who appeared in its open doorway. She smiled back at him, without speaking. For a moment those two were alone in their own world. Then the woman looked at Annie, and asked a question. Sahnko answered her, while he busily untied the rope that still fastened Annie to him.

The woman held out her hand to Annie, and smiled, but more timidly than before. "Aymso," she said. She helped Annie down, and stood for a moment holding her hand. "Li'l girl. Mine," she said, and smiled wonderfully.

The woman was short, no taller than Annie herself. Her face was as brown and her hair as black as Te-Ata's, but there the similarity stopped. Where Te-Ata had been tall and slender, this woman was square and chunky; even her head was blocky, and set solidly on her shoulders. Her hair was unbraided, and hung loose around her shoulders and across her back. It was parted in the middle, with a red line painted along the parting. She wore a dot of red paint on either cheek.

Sahnko's wife wore a buckskin dress, with open, deeply fringed sleeves. The dress was old, and it was stained here and there, but it was not dirty. Annie wondered dimly how the woman could keep her dress soft, and as clean as it was.

Around her waist Sahnko's wife—should she be called Mrs. Sahnko, Annie wondered—wore a stiff rawhide belt. A sheathed knife and a cluster of small rawhide pouches swung from the belt, over her right hip. Again Annie wondered, this time what the bags were for or could contain. There were narrow silver bracelets on the woman's wrists, narrow silver rings on her fingers, small silver pendants hanging from her pierced ear lobes, and a strip of leather studded with silver buttons swung from the belt below the buckskin bags.

"Li'l girl. Mine," Mrs. Sahnko repeated. Still holding Annie's hand, she led her inside the tipi. They had to step up over its laced threshold, and at the same time stoop to go through the door, and Annie hoped she wouldn't have to get out of the place in a hurry.

All of a sudden, Annie was so tired she could hardly stand. She looked around the inside of the tipi, but she could never be sure that she saw it clearly that time, or if she thought she remembered things that she learned afterward.

It was cool inside the tipi, in spite of the little fire burning in a hole that had been scraped in the center of the earth floor. The buffalo hide tipi cover was rolled up all around, so what coolness there was in the mid-June morning flowed under it, across the floor. Heat and smoke from the fire rose straight up and out, between the tipi flaps above Annie's head. The tipi was for all the world like a chimney.

The interior of the tipi was rather bare. There was no furniture of any kind that Annie had been used to. A little stand had been built of sticks just inside the door, on the left of the opening. There were brass kettles and wooden bowls, gourd dippers, and some spoons, which looked as if they had been made of cowhorn, piled on it or stacked around it. Another brass bucket, standing near the door, held water, and a gourd dipper.

At the far back of the tipi were two cot beds made on wooden frames, with painted willow-rod headrests. The cots were covered with painted hides, and stiff envelope-like cases of painted rawhide were piled on and under the beds, like cushions. There were some on the floor beside the cooking stand, and there Mrs. Sahnko sat down.

The door of the tipi faced east, and the morning sun came in to brighten the interior. Sahnko walked around the curve on the south, past the water bucket and cooking utensils, behind his wife, and sat down on the bed which directly faced the door. The second bed was to his right. He motioned with his lips for Annie to sit there.

Meanwhile, Mrs. Sahnko got busy. She pushed the ends of the logs of the cooking fire closer together, and blew on them. She dropped a handful of dry cottonwood bark on the resulting glow. A little flame started up. She hung a brass kettle over the fire from a tripod of sticks, and soon the contents of the kettle began to boil.

While the food heated, Sahnko's wife brought him the water bucket. With the gourd dipper he poured water into his hands and rubbed his palms together. Then he dipped more water and splashed it over his face and head. He drank from the dipper, and passed it and the bucket to Annie. She washed her hands and face, and drank deeply of the water. It had a strange, slightly bitter taste, as if soda had been stirred into it.

A boy about Annie's age stuck his head inside the tipi door. He fired a question at Sahnko, who nodded his head as he answered. The boy vanished as if a conjuror had magicked him away, and Sahnko smiled at Annie.

"Horse. He take," Sahnko said.

His wife, who was kneeling beside the fire, turned her head, and spoke to him over her shoulder. Sahnko replied to her.

"An-nie Don-o-van," he said. His wife repeated the name, then shook her head. She brought wooden bowls and horn spoons, and the bucket of stew, and set the food on the floor before her husband and Annie. Sahnko filled his bowl with stew; then took a little of it in his spoon and laid it on the floor beside the fire. He bent his head, and his lips moved silently. Why, he's saying a Grace! Annie thought.

She imitated him. Putting food on the floor beside the fire seemed a strange thing to do, but as she did it she clearly heard Mother's voice speaking to her.

"A lady does what is expected of her, Annie." Mother had said this from the time Annie could remember her saying anything. "Always keep that in mind. Do what you see the people around you doing when you are in a strange place. Then you will at least look polite."

"You'll never get into trouble doing that," Father always added.

The stew tasted wonderful to Annie, after four days of yellow meal. Sahnko had shown her the mesquite bushes, with long beans filling and ripening on them, as they rode. Then he had made motions of pounding.

[42]

Annie gathered that the meal was made of pounded mesquite beans, and she knew it was good food and filling, but it hadn't satisfied her the way the stew did.

She ate two big bowls full, and then suddenly she was so sleepy that she felt her head jerk forward. Sahnko's wife took Annie's arm and turned her around, and she lay curled up on the narrow bed and everything stopped happening.

It was broad daylight when Annie wakened again. Sunlight was still coming in through the door to the east. She couldn't have slept long, she decided, or the sun would be on the other side of the sky.

Annie sat up, and looked around her. The tipi was empty. She could hear people talking outside. Her head no longer ached, although it felt light on her shoulders. She got off her bed, went to the door, pushed the flap aside, and peeked out.

Mrs. Sahnko was nowhere in sight. Sahnko stood talking to the boy who had taken care of the horse. As soon as Sahnko saw Annie, he stopped talking to the boy, and called, "Maa!"

Mrs. Sahnko came running from behind the tipi. She looked younger and happier than she had when Annie went to sleep, and she was smiling.

"Mah-tone," Maa said to Annie. "Mah-tone shahn." She drew her open hand, palm upward, across her stomach, and looked a question.

[43]

Annie nodded. "Hun-gry," she said. They were work-ing very hard to understand each other. Annie followed Maa into the tipi. Maa pointed to the water bucket and the dipper, and then to the door. Annie picked up the bucket, and went outside the tipi to wash.

When she came back inside there was a wooden bowl filled with food waiting for her. It was dried meat, pounded fine, and mixed with fruit that looked dark, and tasted sweet like raisins. Annie tried to figure out what the fruit was, and finally decided it must be dried wild plums or grapes.

Maa laid her cheek on the palm of her hand, and closed her eyes as if she were sleeping. Annie nodded, and when Maa opened her eyes, she nodded again. Maa pointed to the sunlight, and held up two fingers. Annie stared at her in disbelief. She couldn't have slept to the second day! But Maa repeated her sleep sign and held up the same two fingers. Annie decided that it must be true.

After breakfast, Maa reached under a third bed, which she must have set up while Annie slept, and brought out one of the rawhide envelopes, painted in soft colors, and tied with buckskin strings. She laid the case on the bed, and undid the fastenings; then she turned back the stiff sides of the case. From it rose a soft smell, part cedar, part sage, and part something else that was sweetly fragrant.

Maa lifted out a new, soft, fringed buckskin dress, and

[44]

laid it on the bed beside the case. Then she took out a pair of high buckskin boots. Their soles were rawhide, and the tops were deeply fringed. Maa sat back on her folded legs on the floor beside the bed, and beamed at Annie. She pointed with her lips from Annie to the clothes, and back again.

These were to be her own clothes; Annie understood that. She had taken off the battered wires of the hoop before she ate the previous morning, and now stood in the rags and tatters that had been her undergarments. It would be good to be decently covered again, although the buckskin looked as if it would be warm for summer and there were no underclothes. Perhaps Mrs. Sahnko had made these clothes for her own little girl.

Annie went over to Maa. She picked up the dress, and found it was in two pieces; a skirt and a loose overblouse. She slipped on the skirt, and Maa helped her tie it around her waist with a wide, soft buckskin strip. The blouse slipped over her head and Maa let it hang loose without a belt. Annie was cooler than she would have dreamed she could be.

But she was going to need help with the boots, she could see that. They were all in one piece, so they had to be fitted over her feet and up her legs an inch at a time. It was almost like fitting gloves over the fingers and palm of her hand. When the boots were finally on, with Maa's help, Maa tied them with buckskin garters, and turned

[45]

the tops over, so the fringes swung around Annie's ankles. She stood there dressed like any other Kiowa girl and she felt free and happy in her new clothes.

Now Maa handed her a bunch of coneflower heads, with their stems tied tightly together. She pulled the bristly dried seed sheaths across her own black shiny hair. Annie unbraided her hair, and let its red tangles down over her shoulders. She tried to brush it with the coneflower heads, but it was a useless effort. Maa came to the rescue. She separated the strands, almost hair by hair, and brushed each one by itself. Bit by bit Annie's curls sprang back into place. Annie was shocked at herself. Why, it was almost a week since she had even thought of unbraiding her hair, let alone brushing it! It must look a real mess.

When Maa had finished brushing, she parted Annie's hair along her scalp, front to back, with a little stick. Then she stood off and looked at Annie, shaking her head at the curls, which were already threatening to tangle themselves together again. Annie laughed for the first time, reached up, and began to braid the hair. Maa watched her, interested, as if three-strand braiding were a new and strange thing to her.

By the time Annie was dressed, and the ends of her braids were securely tied with narrow buckskin strings, Sahnko entered the tipi. He looked at Annie, and smiled as if he were pleased. "Li'l girl. Mine," he said, and Annie felt sure he was telling her she was the kind of little girl that Sahnko was glad to have.

There was a sudden babble of noise and excitement outside the tipi; people were calling to each other across the camp, children shrieked, and dogs barked frantically. Then a single man's voice rose above the racket. Everything stopped, while people listened to the camp caller.

"Come on," Sahnko said to Annie. "We go." He was not separating his words with as much effort as he used to, Annie noticed. They left the tipi. The caller sat on his horse near by, calling out something over and over.

Maa motioned to Annie to come with her. Together they stacked the rawhide envelopes in a pile by the tipi door. Annie fitted the brass kettles into one another. She looked at the one that held the water, and picked it up. Before Annie could empty the water on the floor, Maa handed her a limp piece of leather, and made a pouring motion. Annie carefully filled the water bag, and had tied its mouth tightly before she realized that it was made from a cow's stomach, emptied and scraped, and washed clean.

Now Maa lifted the heavy buffalo robes off the beds, and began to fold them. She shook her head when Annie tried to help her, and pointed with her lips to the beds. Now that the covers were gone, Annie saw that the beds were made with willow-rod supports. The withes were strung together side by side with sinew, and the flat mats were tied to upright forked poles at the heads and feet of the beds. Annie unfastened the buckskin thongs that held the mattresses in place, and rolled up the mats. Maa pulled up the forked sticks, and laid them aside, with the side rails. Then she showed Annie how to bind the parts of each bed together.

Sahnko called to them from outside. They went out, and found him waiting for them with the horses. Four wore packsaddles, and two others had high-pommeled rawhide saddles, almost like chairs.

Maa reached up and took one pole that supported the tipi ears. She lifted the pole free, and laid it on the ground. Then she took hold of the pole on the north side of the door, to which the main ear was tied, and began to walk around the tipi, holding the pole upright before her. As she went, she rolled the tipi cover around the pole she held, leaving the support poles bare.

Maa untied the cover from the pole, and drew the pole out of the bundle. Then she caught the end of the rope that tied the support poles at the top, and was twisted around the one at the south side of the door. She unwound the rope from the pole, gave it a sudden jerk and a twitch, and the rope flew away from the poles, leaving them supported only by their leaning against one another.

Finally, Maa separated the twenty-four tipi poles into threes, and tied one set of three on either side of each packsaddle, with their thick ends trailing on the ground behind the horses. On one set of poles Maa piled the folded tipi cover. On the other she set circular racks, their bent willow frames laced together with rawhide netting. On these she packed her cooking utensils, their bedding, and the rawhide cases, lashing each load in place with braided rawhide rope.

Maa swung herself up into one of the high-backed saddles, and Sahnko helped Annie into the other. The stirrups hung on either side, and he drew them up until they fitted Annie's legs comfortably. A horrid realization came to her! She was going to have to ride astride! The last time she had ridden any way but sidesaddle she had been six years old and had climbed on a horse behind Bud. Mother had her down in short order, explaining grimly about ladies and not showing their legs.

Well, Maa and all the other women around them were riding astride, with folded deerskins laid across their laps and hanging down to cover their legs, and Annie supposed she could do it too. Once she had settled herself into the high saddle, she was surprised to find how comfortable it was.

All around them, other families had been working to take down their tipis and load their horses. Some women had big dogs, loaded with small drags and packs, like the horses. Before noon the whole village moved out onto the prairie, traveling northeastward, around the end of the mountain range and out onto rolling high-plains country.

[49]

They traveled for four days, most of the time going north. At first, with all the calling and excitement before the camp was packed, Annie thought the soldiers might be coming for the raiding party. Perhaps they would take her back to Texas—back to her own people! Annie hardly dared think it to herself.

Then she had been too busy helping Maa with the loading to consider anything but the work she was doing. By the time they were on their way, and she thought of the soldiers again, they were on the rise at the end of the hill, and she could look out to the south, the direction from which she and Sahnko had come to the camp. There was nothing in sight anywhere; no movement in the world except that of their own camp. Annie gave up thinking. If she thought, she would only make her heart hurt worse than ever.

All four days they rode at an easy walk. No people who were frightened and running would travel like that. There was a holiday air about the caravan. People were happy; they spoke gently and kindly to one another, as Annie could tell from the tones of their voices. Men and women alike smiled at Annie, and at the other children. The old people and the very small children rode on the drag loads, but everyone else rode horseback.

The young men, riding outside the compact group of women and children, raced their horses around the slowly moving camp. Sometimes a young man drummed on his saddle horn with his bow, and all the men would begin to sing. Even the older men, riding sedately behind the drag horses and the loose herd, would take up the song and sing it deep in their throats.

The prairies were green around them, and studded with gaillardias and coneflowers. Orange milkweed flamed on the uplands, and the green-and-white of snow-on-the-mountain danced in the lower rolls of land. Meadow larks darted up before the horses, their song rocketing ahead of them, and the yellowhammers and flycatchers watched from the trees. High overhead hawks coasted the air currents, wings unmoving except for tilting to retain their balance. And once Maa cried out, and pointed to the largest bird Annie had ever seen. It rose, clumsily flapping, from a pile of dead sticks in a high tree, but as soon as the bird was free of earth it swung above them in flight more graceful even than the hawk's. It was an eagle.

Even with all there was to look at, Annie would still have been lonesome and homesick if she had had the time. The tipi had quickly become home, and home had quickly vanished again. At night they camped in the open, and the warm moon rose over the prairies, a little fuller with each night that passed. At first sleeping outdoors frightened Annie; she had never done it before. On the trip west, she and Mother and Katherine always slept in the wagon. But she learned to like lying on the prairie turf, and saying good night to one star after another, until her eyes closed and she was asleep.

During the daylight riding hours Annie was too busy to feel anything but interest. Other children rode beside her, and tried to talk to her then, or when they all stopped to rest and eat at noon. Late in the afternoon, when the women were busy cooking and preparing for the night, other groups gathered around her. They talked and talked, and from listening and imitating them, Annie began to learn a few Kiowa words.

It turned out to be a hard language to speak. She had to click her tongue against the roof of her mouth sometimes. At others, she learned to make a noise deep in her throat, almost as if she were clearing it. And if she didn't make these strange noises just right, everybody laughed. They laughed even harder until she learned that some words went up and down in pitch, and when and how to change her speaking tone. Annie always had hated to be laughed at. She struggled with Kiowa, trying each word over and over, in order not to make mistakes.

The boy who took care of Sahnko's horses taught her most words. He rode beside her sometimes, pointing to things and saying their names over and over. That was how she learned that the tipi was called "Do." When someone gave her something she was supposed to say, "Aho." "Aimso," the first word Maa had spoken to her meant, "Get down," but people used it whenever they

[52]

greeted their friends. "Baysaw," which Maa and Sahnko said when someone visited their camp, meant, "Sit down." "Maa" seemed to be the word for any grown woman, not just for Mrs. Sahnko. "Mahtone," and "Mahtone shahn," which Annie had thought at first was her own name, just meant "girl" and "little girl."

Everything and everybody in this moving world had a name except Annie Donovan, whose English name was never spoken. Sahnko and Maa acted as if they didn't hear her when she pointed her finger at herself and said her own name, over and over. She wasn't going to be called Annie, that was clear. And she hated being called just "girl," as if she were a thing.

The boy said his name was Guey Konegya; he could not tell Annie what it meant. He was a nice boy, if you liked boys. He tried to be friendly, and he was the only one of the children who was Annie's age; the others were older or younger.

Most of the time Annie thought Guey Konegya just curious about her. But even having someone take that much interest in you helped when you were among strangers, and afraid to let yourself think for a moment about the people you really loved most in the whole world, and what could have happened to them.

Every night, before she said good night to the stars, lying on the robes piled on the ground for a bed, Annie Donovan said her prayers. She said "Our Father" and then she said "God bless." After those, she said a prayer she had made for herself, just, "Please let me find them again, God. Dear God, please let me find them again." And then she turned over and went to sleep—fast, before she could think.

Chapter Four

A New Friend

They came across the roll of the prairies in the late afternoon, and topped a low rise. Suddenly all the Indian world seemed to be spread before them. The river made a deep bend, more than a mile across the bow of the curve. Trees grew along the banks, and framed a great circle of tipis, brush arbors, and straight-sided Army tents.

All the dwellings were set facing the center of the circle. Inside the ring was a circular lodge, open-sided, and roofed with willow boughs. The lodge faced east, and directly opposite it, on the eastern perimeter of the circle, was a gap in the ring of tipis, like a door.

From the lodge came a mingled sound of whistles shrilling, men and women singing, and a dull beating, like that of a faraway muffled drum. Annie listened to the noise, and wondered what it was all about.

For a moment they all sat, waiting and watching. Then Maa jerked her horse forward, and Annie's followed. They rode around the south curve of the circle, as if they were going around the inside of a tipi. At the west end, where two tipis had been opened out and spread over a double set of poles to make an open shade, a group of horsemen waited for them.

These men were painted yellow from their waists to the tops of their heads. Each wore a new dark-blue breechclout, and, streaming over his shoulder, a long dark-blue sash, decorated with clusters of hawk feathers. Sahnko greeted them with his upraised right hand, and a man rode forward. He and Sahnko laid their hands palm to palm for a moment, without clasping or shaking them. Then the man signaled Sahnko to follow, and led them to a camping place on the north side of the circle. The inner ring was set solid with the tipis of the earlier arrivals, and they had to put theirs in the second row.

Immediately Maa and the other women went to work. With quick pulls at the knots they unfastened the tipi poles from the packsaddles. While the men unloaded the animals, each woman set up her four primary poles and fastened them together at the top with a tossed noose. She pulled the rope tight, and wound it around and around the pole that would be on the north side of the door.

Now she filled in between the primary poles with the secondaries. She leaned them into the crotch formed by the crossed primaries, and the framework of the tipi was up.

Next Maa unpacked the tipi cover, and fastened the ears to the carrying pole. She walked around the framework, holding the pole upright before her, in the reverse direction from the one she took when she removed the cover. As she went, she unrolled the cover and spread it over the poles.

The tipi was still open at the front. Maa took a set of small sharpened sticks from the pack, and with them she buttoned the front of the tipi together, from the smoke hole down to the top of the door. She drove stakes through holes in the bottom of the tipi cover, securing it firmly to the ground. Last of all she hung the painted door-flap over the doorway, and laid it back against the north side of the tipi. The family was ready to move in.

Under Maa's pointed directions, Annie carried the beds into the tipi, and helped to set them up. She took a rope, and went into the woods along the creek, to gather kindling.

Girls of all ages, and little boys, were ranging through the timber, gathering sticks. They saw Annie as soon as she stepped under the trees, and a curious group gathered around her. At first the children only stood and stared. Then one of the older girls boldly reached out and touched the end of Annie's braid. Annie stood still. Even if the Indian girl pulled the braid, it would not hurt too much, and Annie was as curious about the others as they were about her.

The girls were all dressed much the same way that Annie was. Some had on newer and cleaner dresses than others, and a few were outgrowing their dresses and would soon have to have new ones. Most of the smaller girls wore low-topped moccasins; it was only those Annie's age or older who wore the high fringe-topped boots.

The littlest boys, up to about five, were all bare-naked except for their moccasins, and some of them were barefoot. The older boys wore belts and breechclouts like the men's. Their hair hung long and loose, sometimes straight and smooth, sometimes matted with tangles. That must depend on when they saw their mothers last, Annie reflected, thinking about how mussed up Danny's hair could get when he was out playing. She closed her eyes at the thought.

The girl let go of Annie's braid, and gently stroked the top of her head. She said something to the other children, who giggled. One at a time, almost as if they were afraid of Annie, the other girls examined her hair and her skin, and giggled softly. Some of them glanced briefly at her eyes, and then their own darted away.

There was a rustle and a stir in the bushes behind them. Guey Konegya stepped into the group. He looked at the girls, who still stood feeling and stroking Annie, and they spoke to him. Then he began to talk, and Annie decided that he must be explaining who she was and how she came to be there. At last he stopped.

The first girl took hold of Annie's hand, and asked a question. Guey Konegya answered. After a moment he added a word. "Mahtone," he said.

The girl let go of Annie's hand, and touched herself lightly on the breast. "Beahtonemah," she said, and repeated the name. "Beahtonemah."

One at a time, she went around the circle of children, pointing with her lips as she named each one. When she got back to Annie she smiled, and put her hand on Annie's shoulder.

"Mahtone," she said, and added something that Annie could not understand. Oddly enough, even without knowing what the words meant, she knew Beahtonemah was comforting her.

Now Beahtonemah picked up her own bundle of sticks, and with it in one hand led Annie with the other along the bank. They came to a place where a spring freshet had piled driftwood into a curve of the bank, and soon Annie had gathered enough kindling to fill the loop in her rope. The other children had dropped behind them when they started down-river, so the two girls went back to camp together.

Women were coming and going all around the great camp circle. Smoke from the cooking fires made blue streaks along the light breeze. Maa was waiting for them at the tipi, and she greeted Beahtonemah with a smile and a word. Beahtonemah asked a question.

Maa took hold of Annie's ear lobe, pinching it between thumb and forefinger. Beahtonemah laughed. She pulled at her own ear lobe, and Annie noticed that she—and now she remembered all the other children, both boys and girls

[59]

—wore a string of brightly colored beads hanging from the pierced lobe. Maa must want Annie's ear to be pierced. It would hurt, Annie felt sure. And besides, Mother had always said eighteen was young enough for a girl to begin wearing earrings. Beahtonemah couldn't be that old. Annie shook her head, but nobody paid any attention to her, and she could not protest in words.

Maa motioned to them to go on, and together the two girls walked slowly around the camp circle. Beahtonemah pointed out one thing after another, and named each one for Annie. The dried meat. The drying rack. The buckskin ball she brought out of her mother's tipi for them to play with.

Annie wanted to throw the ball back and forth between them, from hand to hand, but Beahtonemah played ball in a different way. She balanced it on the top of her foot, and kicked upward. The ball flew up in the air, and Beahtonemah caught it on her foot when it came down. She kicked and caught the ball twelve times before she missed. Then it was Annie's turn, and Beahtonemah passed the ball to her. The game was harder than it looked. Annie missed the first time, and Beahtonemah gave her a second chance. Annie tried seven times before she managed to catch the ball on her foot even once.

She had just got the knack of playing, when she saw Maa coming toward them from the tipi. Annie smiled good-bye at Beahtonemah, and ran to Maa. She was beginning to feel safe and sheltered with the Kiowa woman now, especially in the big camp, with all the strangers around. They walked around the circle to their own home. Sahnko and another man were sitting on a buffalo robe spread on the ground before the tipi.

He was a white man! His hair was brown, and getting a little thin on top of his head, like Father's. His eyes were gray, and his skin was as fair as Annie's own. The man looked at her kindly, and held out his hand to Annie.

"Come thee here, child," the white man said. His lips smiled at her, warmly.

Annie obeyed him. She could hardly believe what was happening. Perhaps this man knew what had become of her folks, or could help her find them. That was almost too much to hope for. It was wonderful enough to be with someone who spoke English, and could understand her.

"What is thy name?" the man asked her.

"Annie Donovan."

"Where did thee come from, Annie Donovan? What has happened to thy family?"

Annie pointed her lips at Sahnko. "Didn't he tell you? What did *he* say?"

"He tells me he went with a party of Kiowas and some Comanches on a raid, down into Texas. They wanted to cut the fence wires and kill the cattle, so there would be more range for the buffalo, and they wanted horses. They came to a farm house where there were many

[61]

people gathered, and a great many horses. To get the horses, they set fire to the barn."

"But there was shooting! They shot at us!"

"He says the white men shot back. Then the house caught fire from the barn."

"I guess it could have," Annie said doubtfully—reluctantly.

"Thee does not believe him?"

"I don't know whether I do or not," Annie stated flatly. "It all happened so fast, and I was so scared. I was trying to take care of my little brother and sister . . ." The whole awful moment swept over her mind and flooded it as the tears flooded her face. "Mother," she sobbed helplessly. "Where is my mother?"

The man sat quietly and waited for the storm to pass. Maa turned from the cooking fire and took Annie in her arms. She cradled the girl as if she were a little, little child, stroking her hair, murmuring, and finally wiping Annie's eyes with the sleeve of her own buckskin dress. Annie clung. This woman was not her own mother, but she was all the love and comfort there was in Annie's world just then.

"Sahnko says that he was in mourning," the white man went on, when Annie was quiet enough to hear him. "Their own daughter was about thy age, and she died two years ago, in the smallpox epidemic. They had no other children. As a sign of mourning, Sahnko said that he would never hurt another human being as long as he lived. I believe him," he added in a different voice. "I have great hopes. Sahnko may hear the Lord's voice someday, and be moved by the spirit to become a Christian."

"I heard people screaming," Annie said. "Some of them may have got away, and some may have just been frightened, but some of them were hurt. Maybe even killed!" She drew a deep shuddering breath.

"Let us hope not, child. Let us pray that they all escaped, for they may have done. Sahnko does not remember, so he says. But the Comanches . . . At any rate, Sahnko saw thee run from the house, and trip over the hoop of thy skirt. Worldly gauds have been the downfall of many women, child. Thee should learn from that."

"It was just made over from Mother's old one," Annie protested. "Worldly gauds" sounded so sinful; she didn't believe an old made-over skirt could be that bad.

"At any rate," her new friend went on hurriedly, "he saw thee fall and went to pick thee up. Thee had hit thy head on the ground, and thee was unconscious, but alive. Sahnko decided thee had been sent to him to replace the other child, so he tied thee to him on the horse and brought thee home."

"And he doesn't know where my folks are, or what happened to them?" Annie demanded.

The man shook his head. "He doesn't know. They drove the horses before them, and rode fast away. They are still afraid the soldiers will come and arrest them, and take thee from them."

"What am I going to do?" Annie asked desolately.

"Await on God's good time," the man said. "Thee could have been killed, or captured by someone who did not love and want a little girl. These people want thee for their own, and they will give thee the best they have. Wait. Be patient. In God's time thee will find thy own again."

He spoke with such assurance and such quiet strength that Annie found herself believing him. This was a good man and she could feel his goodness. She sat beside him, comforted and reassured, and suddenly feeling safe again.

"Who are *you?*" she asked presently. "What are you doing here with the Indians?"

"I am a Friend," the man replied. "I am called William George. Once I lived in Philadelphia. God called me there, bidding me to come West, and teach His red children." He smiled patiently. "Who can question the will of God? I came, and I have tried to teach. No man has done me harm, and any of them will feed me and give me a place to stay. A few will even listen to me, and not go away. I have learned something of the language from the children, who are my best teachers, and they let me teach them my language in return."

"One girl has been trying to teach me today," Annie said. "It's the second time somebody has."

"Thee will learn. What faith has thee been raised in, child?"

"We're Presbyterians. I can say most of the Westminster Shorter Catechism."

"And thy prayers? Has thee read The Book?"

"Father—Father always had us say Grace, and say our prayers before we went to bed. Mother read us the Bible until we were old enough to read ourselves. We always read a chapter a day out loud, taking turns. We've been through it twice."

"Does thee remember the Twenty-third Psalm?"

"The Shepherd Psalm?"

"Yes."

"Oh, yes, I remember that one. And there is another, 'I will lift up mine eyes unto the hills, from whence cometh my help.' And I know Our Father. I say my prayers when I go to bed."

"Say them all each night before thee sleeps. Never forget. If thee can read, I will bring thee a Book. Be true to thy teaching, Annie Donovan, and thy own will come to thee."

"Couldn't you take me with you? Why must I wait here?"

"I travel far and hard, child, from the Red River north to the Arkansas River, and out on the unmapped western plains. I go wherever there are Kiowas. The life would be too hard for thee. Better remain here."

[65]

"But I want to go! If you travel so far and so hard, we might find my family."

"Thee would be worse off. No, child, stay here and have patience. When I go east again, to the government agency where the Government has a representative to deal with the Indians, I will report that thee is here. He can look for thy family, and send them word where thee is, when he locates them. I will tell him, too, that thee is well, and not mistreated."

"No. Everyone is kind to me."

"They will continue. Sahnko and his wife want thee for their daughter. Do not try to run away, for they will always be good to thee. They have fed and cared for thee; they have clothed thee, and they want thee for their own. If Sahnko says he hurt no person I believe him, for he has never lied to me. Thee can feel safe that thee is not with one who might have done harm to those thee loves."

"That's true," said Annie thoughtfully.

"Thee must remember that thee is a Christian, child, and forgive and love thy enemies. If thee can show them how a Christian lives, thee will help me greatly."

"I'll try. Sometimes I guess I'll forget, but I'll try the best I know how."

"And think about this," William George went on. "Once these people lived wherever they chose in this wide country. They came and went, free as the wind, and no man said them nay. But when the white men came into this land, they put fences across the country and barred the red men from the places where they were accustomed to go."

"Well, you have to have fences if you're going to farm."

"So thee does, but these people knew nothing of farming. They lived by hunting the buffalo, and when farmers came the buffalo and the Indians must go. Now the railroads are building across the Indian country, and they have sent out white hunters to shoot the buffalo so the beasts will not damage their tracks. Soon thee will see buffalo only in menageries and zoological gardens."

"But what will the Indians live on when the buffalo are gone?"

"They will have to change their way of life, or starve. Perhaps some of them will learn to farm or raise cattle. But it will go hard with the older people, who know no other way of life."

"I didn't know about all that," Annie said in a low voice. "Father and everybody we knew called them red devils, worse than Yankees, and not worth the powder and ball to shoot them. I never thought about the way the Indians felt."

"Thee knows now that they are people and they can be kind. They in their turn think that all whites are bad, because cruelty and injustice are all they have received from them. That is why thee must live a Christian life."

[67]

"It's hard to do alone."

"Thee is not alone," said William George sternly. "God is always with thee, thee knows. Sometimes, too, I will be here to give thee what little help I can."

"I'll try," Annie promised.

"Thee is still a little girl; thee can't be more than ten. But thee has a Scotch-Irish name and a Scotch-Irish look, and I think the Scotch-Irish stubbornness to go with them. Make up thy mind, and thee can do anything thee wishes."

"And will you and the agent keep on looking for my folks?"

"That I promise thee."

"And"—Annie hesitated a moment—"it's about my name," she said with a rush. "I don't have one here. They don't call me Annie. Maa calls me Mahtone, but the other children laugh. It means little girl, any little girl."

"They will call thee that until thee is given a real name."

"Are they going to give me a name?"

"Oh, yes, soon. In the next day or two, while the Sun Dance continues. That is when they name babies, and I suppose they will name thee at the same time."

"What is the Sun Dance?"

"Thee has seen the willow arbor in the middle of the camp? In that they hold their heathen rites of worship of the sun. The Kiowas all come together for the Sun Dance, each midsummer. After it is over they scatter to their band camps for the rest of the year. Thee will not see so many Kiowas together in one place again until next summer's Sun Dance."

"But why do they name people at the Sun Dance?"

"So that their names will be known. All the Kiowas will be told you are now the daughter of Sahnko and Haynday Mah."

"Is Haynday Mah her real name?"

"That is her name. *Haynday* means to tell a story; *Mah* means a woman, and is the ending of every woman's name."

"What does Guey Konegya mean?"

"Black Wolf, or Wolf Black, in their order."

"And Sahnko?"

Again William George smiled. "Thee knows the cactus—the prickly pear? The one with flat green leaves? Now it is covered with purple fruits. That is his name, Prickly Pear." He gave Annie a little hug. "Now that is enough deep talk for a little girl."

"Just one more. Beahtonemah."

"Spear Woman. She is called that because of her grandfather's way of fighting on foot, with a spear."

"Why not Beahtonemahtone?"

"That would be correct, but it would be too long for any girl. So the name is shortened."

[69]

"I see."

"Now go and play with the other children. Grow and get strong. Don't worry too much about thy people; they are in God's hand. Say thy prayers and have faith that they are safe. I will try to find out all I can for thee."

"Thank you," said Annie.

Chapter Five

A New Name

There was a lot to look at in the Sun Dance camp. People came and went among the tipis and around the circle, drifting across the trampled yellow summer grass like cloud shadows moving over the prairies.

The horses were driven out to pasture in the mornings, and back to the picket lines that rimmed the camp in the evenings. Morning and evening the boys ran shouting behind the horses. The boys were not supposed to let the horses run, but when the horses just accidentally started running, the boys seemed to have a hard time stopping them.

Every morning early, a group of men and boys, their bodies coated with red mud from the river and their hair pulled up and tied in red-plastered horns above their foreheads, burst shouting through the camp. As soon as they heard the Mudheads coming, the women scooped up their dried meat, their staked hides, their water and cooking buckets—whatever was outside the tipis—and ran inside with their belongings.

"Bring! Bring!" Maa cried to Annie the first day, and

Annie obeyed her, just in time. The women in the camp next to theirs were not so quick. Those women spent the rest of the day salvaging what they could of their dried meat from the ground, and brushing the mud off their partly dried buffalo robes. Some of their brass buckets were only dented. Others had holes in them, and had to be lined with rawhide to be used for water buckets.

On the second afternoon that she and Maa and Sahnko were part of the great Camp Circle, Annie heard a noise, and looked out of the tipi door. There was a stir and a rush on the north side of the circle, opposite her. She peered over, to see what was causing the excitement. The Mudheads had stormed through the camp early that morning, so that couldn't be the reason the people were milling around.

The crowd clustered about a big painted tipi. Annie remembered that it was there that the band leader, Dohawsan, had his camp. All the older men gathered at Dohawsan's camp every afternoon, and his wives prepared a feast for them. After the old men had eaten their meal, they sat in the shade of the brush arbor and smoked and talked endlessly.

Now the crowd parted, suddenly. Annie glimpsed the group of riders around which it had clotted. Men in blue uniforms! Yankees! Her stomach stood still, and then bumped down toward the toes of her moccasins. She felt sick—sick the way she had felt when she opened her eyes, and found herself on horseback, tied to someone she could not see.

The Yankees had run them all out of Tennessee. Father had said that the only way to get away from the Yankees was to go West. The Donovans and their friends had gone, and left their homes and everything else dear to them behind. Later, when the Indians were raiding into Texas and killing their cattle, Father had said that the Donovans might have to ask the help of the blue coats after all, although he didn't want anything from them.

Here were the blue-uniformed troopers, riding into the Kiowa camp, just as Annie had begun to settle down and feel safe there. All her old fear returned. This was the only home she had now. If the troopers took her away, she would just naturally die from fright and worriment—she just knew she would. She couldn't be safe from them anywhere, with the forked red-and-white guidon, with a Roman X on it fluttering at the head of the troop, and their tall gray horses, all alike. Some of the troopers were white, but most of them were Negroes.

Heedlessly, Annie turned, and dived into the back of the tipi. She charged straight across the floor, swerving a little to the left of the fire, but taking no time to go around the inner curve, or stop at her own place as she should.

Maa looked up from her cooking, and simply stared at Annie. Annie was sure she was going to be scolded for her rudeness, but Maa took one look at her face, and went to the tipi door. She looked out and across the circle for a moment, and gestured to Annie to stay where she was. Annie crouched against the back wall, waiting, until Maa came back with Sahnko.

Husband and wife talked together for what seemed like a long time. Even if Annie could not understand a word they said, she knew they were talking about her from the way they glanced at her from time to time. All she could do was wait until their talk ended. Then Maa came over and put her arms around Annie. She held her tight, comfortingly.

Why, she knows I was scared, Annie thought.

"You. Mine," Maa stated.

"You. *Ours,*" Sahnko said with additional emphasis. "You stay. Us."

"I'll stay," Annie promised. She clung to Maa. "You won't let them take me, will you? You won't let the yellow-legged Yankees steal me, will you? I'd rather be a Kiowa than go away with them." She forgot they couldn't understand her.

"We keep. Wait," Sahnko assured her. He left the tipi.

The talk and movement and excitement in the camp seemed to go on forever. The troopers went from tipi to tipi, talking with every family. Annie could hear a man speaking first in halting English and then in quick Kiowa. He must be translating for the soldiers.

[74]

At last the riders drew rein in front of Maa's tipi. Already Annie had learned enough about Kiowa good manners to be shocked by men who rode among the tipis and the arbors, stirring up the dust. Well, what could you expect from Yankees?

She heard Sahnko question the interpreter. She heard the man reply; then Sahnko's short, snapped answer in his turn.

"He say he got no li'l girl," she heard the interpreter report.

"We had word that a white child was seen in this camp by the Wichitas yesterday," the white man said abruptly. "Orders are to find her and bring her in."

Sahnko asked a question.

"He say, what li'l white girl's name?" the interpreter translated.

"Tell him I have a list of ten children who have been stolen in the past year. She could be any one of them."

"He say, how ol' she was?"

"They range in age from four to eighteen."

Again an exchange in Kiowa. "He say he got no four year ol', got not eighteen year ol', not been see li'l white girl long times. Got li'l girl his own."

Annie had to smile, scared as she was. Sahnko wasn't *really* lying, she supposed. She wasn't four and she wasn't eighteen. Sahnko was too polite to look at her when he spoke to her, so he hadn't actually seen her. He claimed her for his own little girl in front of everybody, and had, right along. She'd asked him not to let the Yankees get her, and here he was, lying to save her, almost, as if he had known every word she said.

"No white child here, then," the white man said. "All right. We've been the rounds. Somebody's lying, but there's no telling who. Could have been the Wichitas, trying to make trouble. We've been the rounds. Forward —Hoh!"

Annie heard the horses thud away at a trot. That was no way to treat people, she thought. If you insisted on riding among the tipis, the least you could do was ride at a walk, without stirring up all that mess of dust. But what could you expect of Yankees?

Sahnko reentered the tipi. Maa let go of Annie, and looked at him. "She safe," he said in English, so Annie could understand. Then he spoke to Maa, urgently, in Kiowa. Maa nodded. She began to get their noon meal ready. Annie helped her, never asking why they cooked inside the tipi that day, instead of outside as they had before. Maa didn't want the Yankees to come back and find Annie, that was clear.

Sahnko went out again after the meal had been eaten, He crossed over to Dohawsan's camp, where the older men were gathering as usual. Maa and Annie cleaned up after the meal and then sat down inside the tipi. They seemed to be waiting for something or somebody.

It was warm inside the tipi, even with the cover rolled up. Annie, tired out from the morning's excitement, dozed off to sleep on her bed. She wakened at the touch of Maa's palm on her forehead.

"You. Up," Maa directed her. Annie swung her feet over the edge of the bed and sat up. Maa gestured to her own bed, and Annie's eyes followed her hand.

There, spread out on the buffalo robes, was the most beautiful white buckskin dress Annie had ever seen. With it there was a wide leather belt, decorated with silver disks. From the belt hung a strip of leather strung with more silver buttons. There was a painted buckskin case like the one Maa kept her flint and steel in, and a long sheath with a knife handle sticking up from it. The high-boot moccasins and the shoulders of the dress were painted with matching leaf designs.

"Dress," Maa said, smiling. She motioned to Annie. "You." She sounded as if she had been practising the words to herself, or with Sahnko.

Annie knew how to put on Kiowa clothes now, including the boot moccasins, but Maa seemed to enjoy helping her. After Annie was dressed Maa brought out a small rawhide bag from one of her envelopes, and began taking small, carefully tied buckskin bundles from it. Not one of the bundles was any larger than a thimble.

Maa turned back the buckskin wrapping of one package, and showed Annie the dusting of red paint inside it. She put a red dot on each of Annie's cheeks, and another —a very small one this time—in the center of her forehead.

Now Maa took the stick with which she parted her own hair, and separated Annie's in a straight line from front to back. She brushed the hair until it sparkled, and let it lie, loose and curling, over Annie's shoulders.

Maa took up the packet of red paint again. She looked from it to Annie and back, shook her head, and reached in the sack for another bundle. This one held yellow paint, and with it Maa drew a line along Annie's parting, from front to back, as she had drawn the parting stick.

When Annie was dressed and ready, Maa made her sit on the bed, and wait and watch while she painted and dressed herself. Maa took her time about getting dressed up. She, too, wore white buckskin, with beautiful designs painted on her shoulders and boots. She put a red line on one side of her part, and a yellow line on the other. The paint showed up beautifully against Maa's black hair. Annie could see the reason why she herself wore only yellow. The red would have been lost against her hair.

At last Maa was ready, with her belt and its pendant, her rings and bracelets, and her long silver chain earrings all gleaming from being rubbed with ashes. Annie sat and stared at her. Why, Maa was beautiful, really! And she looked young and alive and happy, smiling all over, and gentle, too. Annie loved her very much.

Maa beckoned to Annie to follow her. They left the tipi. Sahnko was outside, waiting for them. He was dressed up, too, in bright yellow-dyed buckskin moccasins, leggings, and shirt. He wore a dark-blue breech-clout hanging to the ground front and back. There were long twisted fringes swinging from the shoulders and the elbows of his shirt. His face was painted, with a band of yellow running straight across his cheek bones and eyes, and out to his loose-hanging hair. He was holding four horses by their reins.

While Maa fastened the tipi shut, Sahnko handed the lines to Annie. She hung onto the reins as he turned and left her, although the horses were standing calmly enough. In this midsummer heat they would be anything but fractious, Annie knew.

Sahnko came back, leading a fifth horse—a white horse, with an open hand painted in yellow on its withers. On each hindquarter four black arrows had been painted, with dots strung behind them, marking the track of their flight. The horse's mane was braided with strips of blue cloth, and its tail had been braided and clubbed with blue, with an eagle feather fastened in it.

There was a fine painted robe on the horse's back, but no saddle. Sahnko swung Annie up, and sat her side-saddle on the robe. Maa covered Annie's legs with a painted deerskin.

Finally Maa took the lines of Annie's horse, but left Annie holding the others. With Sahnko pacing ahead of them, they went around the south side of the camp, well outside the circle of tipis. They went on around the western curve, and continued along the northern edge of the camp to the eastern entrance to the camp circle. From there they crossed directly to the entrance of the Sun Dance lodge, opposite the break in the ring of tipis.

Sahnko stopped just outside the door of the lodge. An old man, whom Annie recognized as the camp caller, came to meet them. Sahnko spoke to him. The old man nodded, and faced inward from the doorway. He threw back his head and called.

Annie had heard him call a long string of names that same way, every day since they had been in camp, and had seen men come to the lodge from each section of the circle. He called the people again. and while they did not move, the men in the lodge all sat and listened attentively.

After his fourth call, the old man spoke. He motioned to Sahnko. He nodded his head at Maa. He pointed with his lips to Annie.

At last the crier stopped his speech-making. The drummers, who sat just inside the door, pounded on a rolled-up rawhide. They all shouted together, "Haw!" Sahnko took the reins, and led Annie's horse into the lodge.

It was the first time she had seen the lodge interior. A little bower of green branches was across from her, facing the doorway. Within it, a stone image hung from a tripod of bois-d'arc sticks. Buffalo robes and a strip of blue cloth were spread on the ground before the shrine, and an old man sat beside it, fanning the image with a crow-feather fan.

All around the curving lodge young men sat or lay on beds of sage. Annie could smell its hot perfume even through the mingling odors of dust and horses, and she never forgot that pungent scent.

The young men were stripped to their buckskin breech-clouts and were barefooted. Their bodies were painted white, but on some the white was streaked with the crimson of fresh blood. The blood flowed from gashes on their chests or backs, and Annie could see that the ground at the foot of the center pole was spotted with blood and scattered bits of flesh.

The sight made her sick, and she looked away from the young men. Maa glanced up and caught the expression on Annie's face. Her own grew even gentler, and she laid her hand on Annie's. "They. Pray," Maa whispered.

The young men were quiet now, resting, while older men washed them, put sage packs on their wounds, and repainted them. Whatever sacrifice the young men had made it was all over, and they were being taken care of now.

Sahnko helped Annie down, and took the lines of the led horses. He handed her the reins of the white horse in exchange. He spoke to the caller, and the old man shouted a name.

There was a cluster of old women beside the drummers, and one of them rose in response. She spoke to the caller, and he called out something, four times.

Maa put her hands on Annie's shoulders, and made her bend forward. So quickly that Annie didn't feel the jar of pain until it was all over, the old woman thrust the point of her awl through each of Annie's ear lobes in turn, and thrust a little clean white pointed stick into each of the holes.

Maa guided Annie's hand forward, and they placed the white horse's reins in the old woman's hand. Maa threw back her head, and a wild trilling call sprang from her throat. The old woman cried out, too, triumphantly.

One at a time, four old women were called forward, and each was given a horse. At last Annie stood there in her finery, with Sahnko on one side and Maa on the other, each with an arm about her shoulders. While the crier started on another speech, Annie surreptitiously lifted her fingers to first one ear lobe, then the other. She glanced at the finger tips. There were no bloodstains on them.

When the speech was over they left the Sun Dance lodge, and walked back to their tipi. Sahnko and Maa still held their arms around Annie as they circled the camp. She put her hands behind their backs, and tried to give them each a squeeze.

William George was waiting for them at the camp. His mules, still hitched to his big green wagon, were tied under a nearby tree. Annie had never been so glad to see anyone in all her life.

The Friend got up, and greeted them. He leaned forward and touched the little sticks in Annie's ears.

"So they have given thee a name," he said.

"Is that what happened?" Annie asked. "I didn't know."

"Surely," the Quaker said, smiling. "They have given thee a name and taken thee into their family, as if thee was a little baby. Everyone has seen and knows they love and honor thee, for they have given away their best horses and finest robes in thy name."

"Why did they do that?" Annie asked. Maa and Sahnko went into the tipi to change their clothes, but she sat close by the Friend. He could explain this new world to her, even though she lived in it and he did not.

"So that wherever thee goes, or however long thee lives, people will know thee as generous. If a time ever comes when thee is in need, people will remember and care for thee. Thy parents have promised generosity from thee, all thy days."

"Oh," said Annie. She sat still, thinking about what the man had said. "It's a big responsibility, isn't it?" she questioned suddenly.

"A very big responsibility," William George agreed. "See that thee proves thyself worthy of it."

They sat together without speaking for a while longer.

[83]

Then a thought struck Annie. "What *is* my name?" she demanded.

William George called to Sahnko, and Sahnko came out of the tipi, laughing. "He says he thought thee would at least understand thy own name!" said William, laughing with Sahnko. He questioned Sahnko again, and then repeated after him a long string of syllables. "Thy name is Mawn-saw-tay-nay-mah," he told Annie. She repeated the name until she could say it easily. Maa and Sahnko stood and smiled at her.

"What does my name mean?" Annie queried, when she was sure that she could say it.

"Does thee know the humming bird?" the Friend asked.

A sudden flash of memory blinded Annie's eyes and closed her ears to everything around her. She could see, more plainly than the camp circle or the Sun Dance lodge or the faces looking at her, the white picket fence around their dooryard, back home in Tennessee. The vivid orange trumpet flowers and their green leaves and trailers rioted over the whitewashed boards, and around each cluster of blossoms tiny jewel-bright bodies quivered on wings made invisible by movement. Their sound was so light and delicate she used to have to listen hard to hear it, and yet now it sounded in her ears louder than the drums and singing coming from the lodge.

"I know them," she replied, choking back the tears that threatened to surge from her throat to her eyes.

"Well, that is thy name," said William George. "The Humming Bird Girl. A pretty name. Hayndaymah chose it for thy bright hair and quick movements."

"Oh," said Annie. The tears escaped. "I want to go home!" She wept. "I want to go home!"

"Hush thee!" William George almost ordered her. "This is thy home now. It must be, for thee has no other that we know of. Here thee is loved and cared for as well as by thy born mother and father, and thee must return happiness for the love and care. That is all that anyone asks of thee."

Annie nodded, and slowly smothered her tears. They sat in silence again. Maa built and lighted a little fire, and began to prepare the evening meal. Presently Annie spoke. She felt quieted and comforted, but very tired. She still did not go to change her clothes; she wanted to stay close to William George, for she could talk to him.

"The Sun Dance," she said presently, "why do they hurt each other? There were some men all covered with blood."

"Ah, cruel! To let thee see it!" William George exclaimed. "But perhaps not. Even children must learn there is cruelty in the world, to be righted." He waited a moment, then went on quietly, "They do not torture one another, child. Each man makes his own offering of his life's blood in that pagan rite."

"Why do they want to do that?"

"They are asking forgiveness for wrongs they have

[85]

done, or they are thanking their god, the sun, for good they have received. If thee were very sick, and Sahnko wanted thee to recover, he would vow to dance in the next Sun Dance. And if thee did recover, he would make an offering of his flesh and blood in gratitude."

"How awful!" Annie shuddered. "I wouldn't want to get well, if he did that. I'd rather die than have him hurt himself!"

"Thee will never be a Kiowa, Annie, I am sure. This is one of the many reasons why I need thy help in showing these people how Christians live. They must learn that God speaks in man's heart, in quiet, not in anguished display."

Again they sat without talking, and Annie wondered how William George could do it. All the other grown-ups she had ever known were forever talking. How did she do it herself, for that matter? She liked to talk as well as anybody, and here, where she seldom had the chance, she usually felt as if she needed to, but she could sit quietly with the Friend.

"The Yankees came this morning," she remarked presently. "Did thee know?"

"Thee is learning the plain speech!" William George exclaimed. "Do so, child. It is music to my ears. I miss hearing it." He spoke to Sahnko, in slow Kiowa, and Sahnko answered, also slowly, trying to fit the pace of his speech to that of the white man's.

"He says the troops were looking for captured children," George translated. "They came from Fort Sill, south of here, to hunt for children who have been taken from their homes in Texas and Kansas. Sahnko and Hayndaymah were badly worried. They were ready to adopt thee and name thee, and the ceremony was planned for today, and they were afraid thee would want to go away with the troopers."

"Oh, no!" Annie cried. "I'd never go with them, not with the Yankees! I'd rather stay here and be a Kiowa!"

"Why does thee say that?" the Quaker asked.

"Because they were Yankees! They were blue-bellied, yellow-legged Yankees! They drove us away from home! I'd never go anywhere with them!" She sprang to her feet, and stood facing the Quaker. He sat with a queer, hurt look on his face for a moment; then he smiled at Annie.

"Annie Donovan," William George said, "thee is a child and does not know what thee is saying. Thee does not know these men, and thee has no right to speak badly of them. Remember this, child. I came here from Philadelphia. Worldly men would say that I am a Yankee. And am I not thy friend?"

Annie stared at him for a moment, as the meaning of his words sank in. Then she held out her hand. "Yes," she said at last, "thee is my friend, my truly friend. And I will try never to speak so of anyone again."

[87]

INDIAN ANNIE: KIOWA CAPTIVE

"Take heed that thee does not," William George directed her sternly. Then he smiled. "And now, supper is almost ready. Change to thy everyday clothes, like a good girl, and help thy mother."

Chapter Six

Growing Up

Annie and Spear Girl were playing the awl game. A piece of white canvas lay on the ground between them. Maa had laid out the game on the fabric, with a trail winding in from the border, crossing little blue streams, and ending at a tipi drawn in the center of the cloth. Most of the trail was red, but in a few places there were blue steps, like the blue streams.

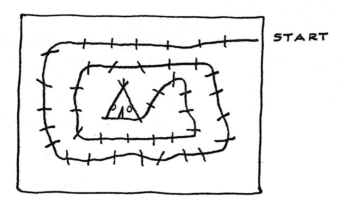

You were supposed to throw your sewing awl at the tipi. Depending on where the point of the awl stuck in the cloth, you moved one of your four plum-seed counters forward a certain number of spaces. If the counter stopped on a blue step. it was out of the game and you had to go on playing with three. The player who got the most counters all the way from the edge of the cloth into the tipi won the game. The two girls were about evenly matched.

"That's three games for you and four for me," Spear Girl said. She looked up at the sun. "We have time for one more. Then I have to go home. Mother wants some water to cook with."

"Yes," Annie observed, "and that gives you a chance to go down to the spring with the bucket, and hang around, waiting to see if somebody will come along and carry it back for you."

"Well, he just likes to carry the bucket. He hasn't played any flute songs, or anything like that, so he just likes me and wants to help out. He knows my father got killed breaking a horse when I was a little girl, and we haven't any man in our family." She picked up her awl, and threw it at the painted tipi. "I miss. Your throw."

The last six years had been the busiest in Annie's life. She had everything to learn, and much work to do while she was learning.

First there was the language, of course. Kiowa became a little easier as you learned it and grew accustomed to hearing and speaking it, but Annie still struggled with the words, and she still made mistakes. Of course, people had stopped laughing at her now. Sahnko had told some of his friends that unless you learned a language when you were a baby, you would never speak it perfectly. Look how hard English was for intelligent Kiowas to speak, and look at some of the things William George said, in all innocence, because he didn't know how to make Kiowa sounds!

Annie had had to learn how to live in a tipi. There were the strictest rules for politeness—what Mother used to call etiquette, at home. You never looked directly at anybody. You never pointed with your fingers, only with a jerk of your lips and chin. You always sat in your own place in your own tipi, but you sat where you were instructed to when you went visiting. And you never knocked on a tipi door, or struck the side of the cover; you stood outside and called your name, and waited to be invited in.

At home, when there were just Maa and Sahnko and Annie, they ate their meals together. But when they went visiting, or when they had company, the men ate first. After they had finished eating and settled down to smoke, the women and girls filled their bowls, and sat and gossiped over their meal. The "Ladies First" rule that Father enforced was not observed here.

Cooking over an open fire wasn't hard for somebody who had learned to cook on a hearth. Annie got the trick of it in no time. Her problem had been learning to eat food after she had cooked it.

The Kiowas had no corn bread, no hot biscuits, not even any yeast-raised bread. Annie never saw milk or butter any more. She missed sweet potatoes, and the clear white of summer squash, and poke greens in the springtime, for now the only vegetables she ate were the wild plants she and the other girls gathered. There were wild onions in the spring, but never at other times. In the Kiowa camp the people ate meat, meat, meat, and everyone thrived on it. Perhaps that was because the only sweets the Kiowas ate were dried fruits and wild honey.

That was the way they lived and ate during the first two years Annie was with them. The band came and went across the prairies, moving as the buffalo herds shifted and the men killed and brought in the game. And then there came a bitter cold winter.

By the following spring the buffalo were gone. The great animals that gave the Kiowas everything: food, clothing, shelter, and a reason for worship, just weren't there any more. The Kiowa world had ended.

Spear Girl's grandmother, who had turned out to be the old lady who gave Annie her Kiowa name, said that one Comanche woman told her that she had seen the buffalo disappear.

The woman was out digging wild turnips on the north slope of the Wichita Mountains when the last herd passed her. They went up the side of the mountain, and the rocks rolled back and the earth opened to receive the buffalo, as a tipi door would open. Dimly, inside the mountain, the woman could see spreading prairies, and green trees growing beside fresh running rivers. Then the last buffalo passed through the door in the mountainside, and it closed behind the herd forever.

Annie came home, and told Sahnko the wonderful story. Hearing it and telling it made shivers run up and down her back. Sahnko shook his head as he listened. His mouth moved as if it would like to smile, but their world was too sad a place for smiling right then with everything that gave life meaning gone.

"It only seems like that because they have gone so quickly," he said. "No, daughter. The buffalo are gone because the white men shot them."

"They wouldn't do that!" Annie exclaimed, her mind flashing back to Father and Bud. "They wouldn't kill more than they could eat. If the buffalo go, we will all starve. Nobody wants to starve other people!"

"The white men don't mind. They are starving us," Sahnko assured her. "We got word today. If we move down to Medicine Water Creek, the soldiers at Fort Sill will give us food and cloth to make clothes. If we stay out, we will have to go hungry."

"The Yankees!" Annie was twelve by that time, and she was still frightened at the thought of the soldiers. "Don't go, Father! The Yankees are the ones who are shooting the buffalo. They're the ones who want to starve us, the same way they starved people at home, during the war."

"I don't know that name for the soldiers," Sahnko replied. "We always call them the red-faced men. Well, I think we should go, and so do the chiefs. We have to go. If we don't go voluntarily, they will send troops here to make us. There are soldiers out all over the plains, rounding up Indians and taking them into the forts and agencies."

And so, of course, they had gone. When the band reached Medicine Creek, north of the fort, they put up their tipis and made a permanent camp, like the camp they had lived in for two or three months at a time during the winter.

A white man, not a soldier, counted them in. Each head of a family reported the number of persons he represented, and received a stack of tickets for each person. Twice a month they all went to the fort.

When they got there, the men turned in one ticket for each member of a family. The soldiers opened a corral gate, and let steers loose, one at a time. The men, on horseback, ran down the cattle, and slaughtered them as if they were buffalo. It made the meat tough, but Maa said tough meat lasted longer and fed more people than soft. Annie felt as if she were leaning into it with her teeth.

Once or twice the agent distributed cloth to the Indians. The fabric was in bolts—whole bolts, like those in the store at home. The women hoarded theirs, but some of the young men were not so careful. They fastened one end of the strip of cloth to a saddle horn and galloped wildly across the prairie, with the cloth streaming after them, By the end of the day, there wasn't an inch of that material that was whole.

The soldiers also issued flour, coffee, sugar, lard, and bacon to the Kiowas. Then it was Annie's turn to be important. Few Indians had seen coffee up to that time, and the women thought you were supposed to boil up the green beans, and cook and eat them the way the Wichitas did the beans that grew in their gardens. Annie knew how to roast the coffee, and to pound it fine with a stone-headed hammer.

Maa and the other women had never seen flour or lard before, and did not know what to do with them. Annie showed them how to fix flour and lard dough with salt and water, and how to bake biscuits. She remembered how Sadie used to pound and pound her dough to make it rise, but only after Annie had tried wrapping the dough around a stick and baking it over the fire. You broke your teeth on *that* combination a few times, Annie decided, and you were ready for anything.

Annie beat the dough till her arms ached, but she beat it light. When she pinched off her biscuits, she put them in a cast-iron dutch oven Sahnko got her at the trading post when she asked for it. Then Annie put the lid on the pot, heaped coals over it, and set the vessel in the fire.

[95]

When her dutch-oven bread was baked, Annie was a heroine. All the women came to her to learn how to bake bread.

Annie knew how to slice up the slabs of bacon, and how to fry the meat in the dutch oven. She remembered to save the drippings, and cook with them when her lard was gone. She was busy every day showing the older women how to use foods Annie had eaten all her life. She wasn't surprised when the Kiowas disliked the bacon, and fed it to their dogs. The meat was strong and musty, sometimes even moulded through. It must have been years old!

For a few days after each ration issue, everybody in the camp on Medicine Water Creek had enough to eat. They even had enough to share with visitors who came from other bands, farther away from the fort. The visitors had their own ration-issue days, which did not fall on the same dates as those of Annie's band, so they were all hungry when they arrived.

There were other Kiowas who hated the white men so much that they refused to accept food for themselves and their families, and tore up their ration tickets, or threw them away. They were willing to eat the strange food in Maa's camp, though. When their rations were gone, Annie and Maa and Sahnko lived on tight belts and water again, as Sahnko said. If they were very hungry, they went to visit friends in another band, like everybody else.

[96]

Whenever the people went to the fort to be counted, Annie wrapped herself up in a buckskin robe, so that her coloring could not be seen. She had no mirror, but she knew well enough that the long hair she brushed and braided every morning was redder than ever from the sun, and that the fair skin of her hands and arms was dotted with freckles. Nobody would ever mistake her for an Indian by looking at her!

Maa kept Annie nicely dressed. When their buckskin dresses wore out, and were too frayed and shabby to wear any more, Maa cut up one of the worst worn, and made moccasin uppers of it. She made the soles by cutting up one of her beautiful painted rawhide cases. After all, they didn't move around so much now, and didn't need so many cases. Packing boxes from the trading post would do to hold things.

Maa took the moccasins to the trading post near the fort, and swapped them for calico. She made dresses for Annie and herself from the printed cotton cloth, cutting the fabric with her knife on the same pattern as their buckskin dresses. She even left a tab on either side of the dress, at the hem, where the legs of the deerskin used to hang down. Annie slipped into the cloth dress happily. She had almost forgotten how cool and light fabric clothing could be.

Maa used her knife for everything, even after the trader began to stock scissors. It looked funny to see her cutting out a dress with a knife, but she was used to using one and worked more quickly than Annie did with the scissors Sahnko bought her.

Whenever she could, Maa traded bread or sugar to other Indians for buckskins. They could get small ones, a few at a time, from the Shawnees who lived east of them, in the thick woods. The hides were never large enough or strong enough for dresses, and there were never enough of them, but the skins could be used for moccasins. The officers at the fort, Annie learned, liked to wear moccasins in the evenings, after wearing heavy boots all day.

When William George found out about Maa's moccasin business, he spoke to one of the officers. Once a month, the man gave Maa two cowhides, when meat had been butchered for the soldiers' mess. Maa scraped and dried them and made rawhide of the skins to use for moccasin soles.

Her cow-hide-and-deerskin moccasins weren't as good as real buffalo-skin moccasins, and Maa knew it. They were plenty good enough to sit around in, though, and neither the trader nor the officers seemed to know the difference between these and moccasins that would hold up to days of riding or trailing. So Maa's knife flashed, and she and Annie stitched with awls and cow sinew, and the moccasins kept them clothed, and even provided little luxuries.

One by one, the buffalo-hide tipis wore out, like the skin clothing. One by one, the covers were lifted down. cleaned and cut up for dresses or moccasins. And each set of poles was covered with brown canvas, or, if the owner were lucky, with white wagon sheeting. The women were forgetting how to cut skins for tipi covers; they sewed the sheets of cloth together in long spirals.

Some women turned lazy, and refused to go to the trouble of making even canvas tipi covers. They somehow managed to get worn-out Army tents, and they lived in those. The tents had stove-pipe holes in their walls, and no other way to let the smoke out, so the women were hot and uncomfortable when they cooked, but then, the tents were too hot to stay in except in cold weather anyway.

And then one day Annie realized that they had been living in this same place, in the same camp on Medicine Water Creek, for four years, and that she was fourteen years old. She was growing up.

Spear Girl was still her dearest friend, even though she was two years older than Annie. They had stopped playing with dolls made of stuffed prairie-dog skins soon after they moved to the permanent camp. Both girls went on playing kick-ball. Everybody played it, from the oldest grandmothers to little girls who could barely walk.

They went out along the creek together, looking for wild plants and fruits to eat, and bringing food back to camp. One day Spear Girl's mother showed them a wild balm plant, and asked them to look for some of that. When the girls came home with big bundles of the plants, Spear Girl's mother showed them how to strip the leaves from the stems, and then dry and powder the leaves to tie up in cotton bags. Annie felt very grown up with her sachets. She had never used any kind of perfume before. She began putting a few dried balm leaves in the water when she washed her hair with soap weed.

And then, suddenly, it was more fun to sit and talk than to do anything else. The two girls used to go off along the creek, upstream from the camp, to a place where the wild grapevines looped and tumbled from the treetops. How many Kiowa girls, for how many years, had swung in those looping vines, nobody knew or guessed. The surface of the bark was shiny-smooth with the polish of moccasined feet.

Side by side, Annie and Spear Girl stood in the loops and pumped the swings back and forth, or let the swinging die, and slid down on the looped vines, to talk.

Spear Girl's mother had begun making and trading moccasins at the trading post, after she saw how Maa did it. Spear Girl and her younger sister wore calico dresses like Annie's. So the girls could talk about clothes and colors, for there were more colors on the printed fabrics than the Kiowas had dreamed there could be in the whole world.

Spear Girl's mother took her two girls to the trading post, and let them choose the cloth for their own dresses. Maa never took Annie, and for a long time Annie didn't want to go. They were both still afraid that the soldiers would see her, and would want to take her away. Each time Spear Girl went to the trading post, she told Annie about all the wonderful things there were in that place. After a while, Annie yearned to see for herself.

Spear Girl could describe the white-man things, but she could not always name them. Annie had to do that. She taught Spear Girl the English names, as Spear Girl had once taught her Kiowa words. It was from Spear Girl that Annie learned that there were dutch ovens to be had, and "two-knives," which she finally figured out meant scissors. From Spear Girl Annie learned about the round shiny metal boxes that had pictures of strange fruits, and of corn and fish on them. That description meant nothing to Annie. Her mother always put up fruit jam in earthen crocks, and they stored vegetables in the root cellar.

Finally, Annie couldn't stand just hearing about the trading post. The next time Maa and Sahnko got ready to go there, she asked them to take her with them.

"The soldiers come there. They might get you!" Maa cried out.

"No, they won't. They won't know I'm not a Kiowa. I'll cover my head and keep it covered, and I promise I won't speak English. I promise, Maa. And I've just got to see everything! I'm tired of hearing about it and not seeing it. Please, please take me."

Maa and Sahnko exchanged glances. Eventually, reluctantly, Sahnko nodded. "Somebody will see her with us some day, anyway. I'm surprised they haven't noticed her already. Let her go with us. She can't stay hidden forever." He turned to Annie. "You are our daughter," he reminded her. "We want to keep you with us and have you as our daughter always. What will happen if you see white women and their children? Will you want to leave us?"

"No," Annie replied. "My home is here, with you. William George has asked and asked, and he has never found anybody who knew what became of my people, or whether they are dead or alive. William George would find out, if anyone could. He goes everywhere, and everybody trusts him and tells him whatever he wants to know. They must all have been killed that Sunday." She was sad, but she had no tears left now for that long ago day; it had slipped imperceptibly to the back of her memory. "You are my mother and father and I'm going to stay with you."

On a hot summer morning, they all rode over the hill and across the flats to the fort. They rode past the stone horse corral where Kiowas from the northern bands had been shut up. That was the winter Sahnko first made camp on Medicine Water Creek, and they began to live there. Annie had forgotten how the people were ashamed and suffering, until she saw the horse corral.

They crested another little slope, and saw the square brown stone blocks of the buildings at the fort. They rode around the parade ground, and along the road leading from it.

The trading post was located south of the fort, in a cottonwood grove by another little creek. There was a

big wooden building, painted red, like a Tennessee barn.
Its familiarity was so strange it startled Annie. What in
the world was a red-painted frame barn doing here?

Kiowas sat on the porch along the front of the store,
smoking, talking, and just looking around them. Maa
and Sahnko greeted their friends, and they all went in.

Inside the building were all the wonders Spear Girl
had described to Annie, and more. There was a whole
case full of needles, and one of different-colored threads.
There were bolts of soft flannelette, and of shiny sateen,
and of brilliantly colored calicoes. There were the tin cans
with pictures on them, but Annie did not need the pictures to tell her that the cans held corn and tomatoes and
sardines. She could read. She had almost forgotten there
was anything in the world to read except the Bible
William George had given her.

Annie stayed close to Maa, following her adopted
mother around the store, looking at the big mirrors that
stood against its walls, and the wooden-backed hairbrushes
and the flat straight fine-toothed combs. Annie had forgotten about all these things, but as soon as she saw them,
she recognized them and remembered their names. She
stopped before a big mirror, when Maa was busy looking
at blue-enamel buckets. Annie let her robe slip back, and
looked at herself.

She saw a girl who was tall enough, and very
straight. The girl was thin, and her freckled face was
narrow, but not pinched. Not pretty, Annie thought,

remembering the smooth rounding of Spear Girl's brown cheeks. But not ugly, either, she decided. The eyes were blue, and not washed-out gray like some of the soldiers' eyes. The girl in the mirror had a smiling mouth. It was a happy, healthy girl's face. There was nothing sour or mean about it.

Behind her, Annie heard a voice say, in English, "Come here, honey."

Annie spun around, to see the woman who spoke in that soft high southern voice, quickly pulling the robe up over her head as she did so. The woman was partly turned away, and did not notice Annie's movement. The speaker was a young woman, and she was bending forward, pulling at a little boy who was determined to climb on a pile of saddle blankets.

"Come here, honey," the mother insisted. "The man doesn't want you climbing all over his things. He has to keep them nice, to sell them. Get down, now."

The little boy turned around on top of the stack and slid down its side. He was such a little boy! His arms and legs were thin, his light hair was mussed and pushed back from his forehead, and a dirt streak blurred one cheek. He looked like Danny when he had been playing up in the barn loft. Annie dropped to her knees, and held out her arms to him.

The little boy stood looking at her soberly. His finger moved toward his mouth, then he dropped his hand as if he had been scolded for thumb-sucking.

"Say hello to the Indian lady, honey," his mother prompted.

Annie still had not spoken, and now the sound of the English words reminded her that she had promised not to. She got slowly to her feet, drew her robe tightly around her throat and up over her forehead to hide her face, and walked across the floor to the place where Maa and Sahnko waited and watched her. Together, without a word, they left the trading post.

After that, though, Annie went to the trading post whenever her foster parents did. They were there one day, camped in the grove beyond the store and waiting for the next day's ration issue, when the trail herd of steers came past from the south.

The cowboys were strung out along the herd, trying to move them quickly past the store and around the post. There had been good rains for the past month, so the ground was not dusty. Looking at the men in the big stock saddles, Annie jumped. One of them was familiar, although she did not fully recognize him. Then she realized that he was Indian, but not a Kiowa. He was someone Annie had known somewhere, sometime, long before, but she could not place him.

That night in bed, just as Annie was dropping off to sleep, the memory returned to her. She saw this man meeting a tall, dark pretty woman in a dooryard, and going with her into a log cabin. What were their names? The woman was Te-Ata, and the man—the man—the man's name was Bill Jim. Perhaps, if she could speak to him tomorrow, she could find out something about her folks.

It wasn't easy. The men were busy around the cattle chutes; there was a lot of shouting and yelling and laughing in deep men's voices. The steers came dashing out of the gates and the Kiowas rode after them, while the cowboys and the soldiers yelled and shouted. At last the final steer had been released, and Annie looked around for Bill Jim.

She found him sitting with some of the other men, with a cup of coffee in his hands. They all stared at Annie. A nice Indian girl didn't come around strange men alone, but Annie hadn't dared bring Maa or Spear Girl with her. She had to take a chance by herself.

She stood on the opposite side of the ring of men, and looked directly across at the Choctaw. Slowly, he raised his eyes from his coffee cup, and met hers. She saw him jump.

"I want to speak to thee," Annie said.

"I don't know you," the man answered, concentrating on his coffee cup again.

"Oh, go on, Bill," one of the others said. "You're lucky, boy. It isn't every day a nice little squaw comes around looking for somebody."

"I know thee," Annie persisted, ignoring the other man, although she could feel her cheeks blazing. "I knew thee a long time ago, down in the Choctaw Nation. I was just eight years old."

The man looked at her again, and got slowly to his feet, staring at her. "What do you want?" he asked.

"I want to talk to thee. Come over here."

The man followed her wordlessly. When they were within sight, but out of hearing of the others, Annie said,

"We came from Tennessee in a wagon, and we camped near thy place. Thy wife's name is Te-Ata, and she was good to us. There were my father and mother, my big brother, and my little brother and sister and me. We had three freedmen. Does thee remember?"

Bill Jim nodded, dazedly. "You—you—ain't no ghost?" he stammered.

"No. Why does thee think I am?"

"They tol' us you was dead."

"Who told thee?"

"Your Maw and Paw, that's who. They came back by two and a half years later, headed for the Cherokee Nation."

"Alive? They were alive?"

"Sure they was alive. I jus' tol' you. But they say you was dead or carried away. They didn't know which."

"Were they all right? Were they well?"

"Sure they was well. They los' about all the stock

they had, but the Indians hadn't bothered the things in their house, so they had enough to sell out and get a couple crow-bait horses and get out."

"What happened to all the other people? There was a crowd there that day."

Bill Jim rubbed his forehead with his knuckles. "Seems like they said . . . I guess they was all right. You was the only one. Killed or carried away, they didn't know which, and they couldn't fin' you, though they tried every way. Reported it to the troops, an' all like that. Your Maw was still grievin' for you."

"Oh!" Annie's cry was low, but it came from all her pain and doubt and fear, to reach her mother, who had suffered the same way, wherever her mother might be. "Where are they?" she demanded of Bill Jim. "Where did they go? Are they still there?"

"I don' rightly know."

"You've got to! You've just got to! You said they were in the Cherokee Nation."

"I said they was *headin'* for the Cherokee Nation," Bill Jim corrected her.

"I've got to go there. I've got to find them."

"Cherokee Nation's a big place," ruminated Bill Jim. He thought, while Annie waited impatiently. "Tell you what," he resumed. "You all right here?"

"Oh, yes. They're good to me. I'm adopted."

"Well." Again he stopped to consider. "You got any money?"

"Money?" Annie never had any money. "Why?"

"You goin' to the Cherokee Nation, you got to have money to get there."

Her shoulders drooped. "I forgot. No, I haven't any money. We—none of the Kiowas have, you see."

"Well. We're going back to south Texas, down on the Brazos. Then we'll bring the last herd up for the season, to Dodge City, Kansas, and scatter out for home. I can go east to the Cherokee Nation, instead of south to the Chickasaw Country. That way I go straight south from there on my way home, and I can look for them along the way."

"Oh, would you do that? Would you?"

"Yes." The one word was all the reassurance in the world to her. "What shall I tell them when I fin' them? Where you be?"

"In the big camp on Medicine Water Creek. They call me Humming Bird. They can find me."

"All righ'." He looked at her hair and grinned. "No bad name for you. I fin' 'em somewhere an' tell 'em." He turned away, and then turned back. "May take a while. Don' worry if it don' happen for long times. Maybe I trail three, four herds before I fin' 'em. You wait. You be patient."

"All right," Annie promised. "I'll wait, and I'll try not to worry." Another thought struck her. "You won't forget my father's name, will you? It's Donovan—Michael Donovan."

Chapter Seven

Making a Life

Then there was another change in the friendship between Annie and Spear Girl. When they went to the spring upstream from the camp for water, one of their mothers, or Spear Girl's grandmother went with them. And on the way back, they often met Black Wolf and his friend, Riding Away.

The two boys were always together, as Annie and Spear Girl were. The boys rode their ponies back and forth from the camp to the fort and home again. They hunted coyotes together, for the bounties the white farmers paid for coyotes' ears. And you could see them any day, riding around the edge of the camp, stopping their horses to talk to other young men, or sitting on them, looking around, just as Annie and Spear Girl happened to come along. They even did some walking, always in the same direction the two girls had taken a little while before.

Annie thrust her awl down at the painted tipi for one last time, and ran out the game.

"You won," Spear Girl said placidly. She helped Annie fold up the painted canvas game sheet—it had lasted them for two years now—and bundle the counters in their little calico bag. "Come on and get your bucket," Spear Girl went on. "It's time to go to the spring for water."

Maa looked up from her cooking when Annie entered the tipi. The autumn evenings were drawing in, and the chill in the air made the fire feel good. Annie held out her hands to it, and then picked up the blue-wool shawl that lay folded on her Army cot. She drew the soft fabric around her. It was lighter and warmer than deerskin.

"Don't stay long," Maa cautioned her. "It gets dark early now. Don't stay out and let the owls get you."

"I won't stay," Annie replied. "We're just going for water for Spear Girl's mother, is all." For the thousandth time she wondered why the Kiowas were so afraid of owls that they would run into their tents and cover the children with blankets if they even heard one hooting. They said owls brought death and bad luck, but Annie had never learned to be afraid. An owl was still just a night-flying bird to her.

"Is Spear Girl's mother going with you?"

"Her grandmother, I think."

Maa's eyes danced. They slid sidewise to the line of filled buckets already curving around the tipi wall. "Maybe someone is planning to take a bath," she said.

[111]

Annie had to laugh herself. "Maybe," she answered. "I won't be long," she repeated.

"Look out for owls and night crawlers," Maa warned as Annie left the tipi.

Spear Girl was waiting with her bucket and she and Annie walked toward the spring. Grandmother trailed behind them, scolding under her breath. They were crazy to go out like this on the edge of the evening. Anything could happen to them. If she weren't a wise old woman, and willing to give up her comfort to take care of them . . . on and on and on.

It took quite a while to fill the bucket. Spear Girl rinsed it out thoroughly. Then she scoured it, inside and out, with clean sand from the creek bed.

"It's really getting dark," Annie said finally, impatiently. "Grandmother won't stay any longer, and our mothers will worry. Come on. Let's go back."

"Crazy, bad girls," the old woman railed. "Just fooling around, waiting for the night crawlers."

It was the second time Annie had heard the word that day. "What's a night crawler?" she innocently inquired.

"If you stay out too late, you'll find out," Grandmother informed her. "A young man who comes crawling through the bushes, to catch a young girl who stays too late by the spring, with nobody to look after her, that's who a night crawler is. We're going back. Come on, now."

"I guess," Spear Girl reluctantly agreed. She stooped to fill the bucket, and, as she straightened up, the flute song began to fill the quickly darkening twilight.

It was a simple tune, just five notes up and five down, with little trills and quavers. The music broke and resumed, like the speech of a boy whose voice is changing. The little tune ran behind them all the way back to camp, in spite of Grandmother's hurrying them along. Annie knew whose flute it was. Only Riding Away played that flute tune. She had heard him practising behind his mother's tipi.

Annie sighed a little as she went into the tipi. She felt lonesome. Spear Girl had someone to play the flute for her, but Black Wolf hadn't even come to the spring to walk back with Annie.

"Did you hear anything?" Maa asked.

"Only a flute," Annie answered. "It played us back to Spear Girl's camp." She laughed. "We didn't hear any owls, if that's what you're worrying about."

"They do worry me," Maa replied quietly. "I heard one in the hackberry tree, over there, while you were gone. He spoke plainly. Bad luck is coming to someone—someone near us."

In spite of herself Annie shivered. She lived on the edge of hope, since her talk with Bill Jim, although she had not mentioned it to anyone. Suppose something happened to some of her folks, before the Choctaw could find them and bring them back! She shook her head.

She was a Kiowa in many ways, but she was not going to take up their superstitions! William George would never forgive her if she did that. The spirit would move him to give her one of his solemn, quiet scoldings, that hurt worse than anything Annie could think of.

Black Wolf did not appear for the next eight days. During that whole time nobody mentioned where he had gone, or the reason for his going. Annie wasn't going to ask anybody about Black Wolf! Maybe Riding Away knew where his friend was, and maybe Spear Girl could find out from Riding Away, but Annie wasn't going to ask them! If he wanted to go off without telling her or anybody else where he was going, that was all right with Annie.

During the week that Annie alternately pouted and moped, Maa didn't ask questions. Maa never asked questions. She went for water during the day herself, but she sent Annie with Spear Girl and Grandmother in the evenings.

"Even with her grandmother around, it isn't a good idea for a girl to go to the spring alone when a young man is playing flute songs to her," Maa explained. "People might think the wrong thing, and then they might get to talking."

People in camp talked anyway, Annie reflected. They

were always talking. Somebody was always making fun of her because she walked back from the spring with her girl friend and nobody played flute songs for her. Annie was sure she had heard the other girls giggle when she walked past.

One girl even asked blandly, "Which one of you is he playing to?" Annie was furious. That girl knew who Riding Away was playing to!

William George drove into camp on the evening of the seventh day that Black Wolf was gone. His mules were drooping in the traces. The mules, the wagon, and William himself were coated with the fine red dust which streamed up from the autumn-browned prairies like flame-stained smoke this dry fall.

This was the time of year for prairie fires. Several times a day Sahnko stopped whatever he was doing, to shade his eyes and peer off to the northwest. Strong autumn winds would drive the flames at them from that direction, if the Kansas farmers started burning off their fields. Annie had never been in a prairie fire, but she had heard about them, and once had seen the night glow, far away. The Washita River had stopped the fire that time, but that had been after a wet summer.

Annie ran to the wagon, now, to meet the Friend. Together they unhitched the mules and, while William went to camp to speak to Maa and Sahnko, Annie led the mules to the pasture and staked them out. When she got back, William was washing his face and hands. Maa handed him a dipper of water when he had dried them, and he drained it gratefully.

"It is dry between here and the Agency," he said when he could speak. His voice was husky. "Dry. If we do not have rain soon, I fear for a prairie fire."

"I, too," Sahnko agreed. "We could have a fire like the one my father used to tell about. It came in the year when the Osages cut off the Kiowa women's heads (1832). It was in the fall, after they moved from the mourning camp, where the women's heads were left stewing in their own cooking buckets."

"Ooh!" Annie shivered.

"Then that fall the smoke went up to the sky," Sahnko continued as if she had not spoken. "It heated the clouds, and the rain poured down like the people's tears, and put out the fire."

"Don't talk about it," Maa said, shuddering. "I was born that year. My grandmother used to tell us about it, how she and the other older women hid in the bushes and kept the children quiet until the Osages had gone away and the Kiowa men came back. I'm still afraid to think about it, especially with that owl around."

Annie didn't want them to get started talking about the owl. William and Sahnko would get into a long philosophical discussion, she knew, and it would end with the Friend's shaking his head and saying that one man's superstition was another man's religion.

"Where has thee been?" Annie asked, in careful English. She used the plain speech altogether now, for William was the only person to whom she spoke in her own language.

"To Fort Sill," William replied.

"What is happening there?" Sahnko inquired, in Kiowa.

"Oh," said William, smiling, "they are very busy there. A new troop of cavalry is coming in next week. No, that is a mistake; it is not a new troop. It is the Tenth Regiment, which was the first to serve at Fort Sill. The ones with crosses on their shoulders. The buffalo soldiers."

"The buffalo soldiers!" Sahnko said, and laughed in his turn. "The black white men! Nah! They can fight, those buffalo soldiers with their short swords! Swish, swish, swish, they swung them at us! They fought to kill. We fought for horses, and to keep score. We learned to fight to kill from them. Those buffalo soldiers are men!"

"Who are the buffalo soldiers?" Annie asked. She had heard the words before, but had never understood them.

"The troopers of the Tenth Cavalry Regiment," William said. "They are Negroes who escaped to the North before or during the war, or were set free by the Emancipation Proclamation. Younger men have joined them since, and most of their officers are white. Kiowas call them the buffalo soldiers because of their thick hair. No fighting men on the plains have ever been more respected than the buffalo soldiers."

Annie sat still for a moment. It was time for her to get up and help Maa prepare supper, and she was going to—in just a moment—but something nagged at her mind, and she wanted to straighten her thoughts.

"Thee is trying to tell me something else," she said shyly.

"Only what I have always tried to tell thee," William answered. "That a man is a man, no matter what color his skin may be. If he lives a good life and respects himself, all other people will respect him too. Someday thee will learn that, Annie."

"These are slaves, who ran away from their homes, and joined the Yankees! How can they live good lives and be respected? How can they respect themselves? They left the people who cared for them and were good to them, to go off and join the enemy. That was stealing!"

"Annie," said William sternly, "I think thee is old enough to learn and remember one thing. That war thee talks about as if it were still being fought is over. Thee thyself can barely remember the troopers to whom thy mother gave water, at thy home; or thy father's return with thy brother. The war meant nothing to thee, of thyself. Thee was not hurt; thee did not starve. None of thy kinfolk died."

"No," Annie muttered, hanging her head.

"As for the slaves who ran away, let me ask thee this. Thee has lived with the Indians eight years now, since thee was a child of ten. Thee is a woman grown. Can thee believe now, after living among men who belong only to themselves, that it is right for one human being to own another's body? No, do not answer me now. Go help Haynday Mah. Think about what I have been moved by the spirit to say." He deliberately turned to talk to Sahnko.

Half Annie's mind was busy with the dutch-oven bread for the next half hour. The other half listened to William and Sahnko. If she kept her whole mind busy with other thoughts, she would not have time to remember what William had told her.

"With more troops coming in, they will need more guides and scouts at the fort," she heard William say. "They are going to hire more young men. They will need interpreters, too."

"Guides and scouts!" Sahnko snapped. "Scavengers!" He spat toward the fire. "Spies on their own people! They are guiding and scouting against the Apaches now. Well, the Kiowas and the Apaches have had their own quarrels for a long time. All the same, I wouldn't show any white man where another Indian is hidden. Guides and scouts! I have no use for guides and scouts!"

"How do you feel about interpreters?" urged William

gently. "Have you no use for the men who bridge two peoples? For the men who make it possible to teach the children and heal the sick?"

"They're different," Sahnko agreed reluctantly.

"You know," William continued, "that there are some whites who wish only good for the Indians. I try to be one of their number. Still, I wish I had an interpreter to help me reach men's hearts and minds. I could do so much more—so much more. If only I had another pair of hands and ears!"

Annie could not put that thought aside. As she helped Maa serve the meal, she really looked at William, and thought about it. He was an old man, sitting there in the firelight. The fringe of hair around his head was white, not brown anymore. His eyes were tired, and the corners of his mouth drooped wearily. He had lost most of his teeth, here where there were no doctors.

William was an old man. Still, when he looked at his friends of years, Sahnko and Haynday Mah, or when he looked at their daughter Annie, his face was gentle, and his smile grew young. All of a sudden a thought struck Annie, and her heart lurched and sank inside her. What if something happened to William? How could she ever go on living without her friend; without her one tie to the world where she lived when she was a child?

"Food is here," Maa said, and placed the wooden dishes before the men.

Both bowed their heads, and they said their different

Graces in their different ways. When William looked up as he finished, directly into Annie's eyes, she thought for a moment that he had seen inside her heart. He must know everything she had been thinking. And it seemed to her in that moment he had answered her bewilderment, and comforted her.

Later in the evening, when she and Maa had eaten their own supper, and when the old canvas tipi was cleaned up, and everything was put away, Annie sat down beside William again. She could hear Riding Away's flute, off in the distance, singing its little five-note song. He must be standing outside Spear Girl's tent, playing to her under the cold stars. The owl spoke from a nearby tree, and spoke again. Annie felt very lonely.

"Does thee think a girl could be an interpreter?" she asked the Quaker, not looking at him.

"A girl?" William repeated. "Perhaps. Or perhaps she could be a teacher, or a nurse. Perhaps she could train other people, both men and women, to become interpreters. That would be even better that interpreting herself."

"I never thought of that," Annie answered thoughtfully. "How does thee think I could do it? Could I really start to teach English to the Kiowas?"

"Why not?" William inquired. "If thee has faith, thee can move mountains. And thee has more than faith, child. Thee has the willingness of the Kiowas themselves. They want to learn to speak English, because they see that they need it in their daily life. Even when thee first came here, most men spoke a few little words. Thee is one of them now, and the Kiowas will be willing to learn from thee."

Black Wolf reappeared at the spring the next evening. The two girls had filled their buckets, and Grandmother was fussing because they were waiting for the flute song to begin before they started back to camp.

Suddenly a shape formed beside Annie, out of the dusk, and a hand reached out and took her bucket from her. Riding Away began his little tune, and he and his song followed them, all of them dancing to it, as the two girls carried Spear Girl's bucket between them to her mother's tent.

After that, Black Wolf walked beside Annie to carry her bucket back to the home camp.

"Are you angry?" he asked her.

"Why should I be angry? I've got nothing to be angry about."

"Well" he paused—"I thought maybe, because I went away without telling you."

"You can go where you please, whenever you please," Annie snapped. They were getting close to the tipi now, and soon she could get inside, away from all this talking.

Black Wolf reached out and caught her wrist with his free hand. "Listen to me, please," he entreated.

Annie faced him. "Don't do that. You hurt. Go ahead and say what you have to say. I'm listening."

"I wanted to tell you why I went away."

"Go ahead. Tell me."

"I went because—because I wanted something. I wanted you more than anything. I wanted to take care of you, the way men used to take care of women. How can I do it now? They used to hunt, and go for horses. Now there is no game, and no place to pasture the horses." He stopped and stood there, looking at Annie.

"Go on," she said, with her head bent.

"So I thought. I thought a long time. There are your friend and my friend. They will get married soon. They are not making any plans about how they are going to live together. I thought, that is wrong."

"Perhaps they have made plans and not told us about them."

"Perhaps. But I thought, I should have a plan before I speak to her. I made my plan, and I went away to carry it out. Will you help me?"

Annie stood without speaking. Something was beating inside her like a dance drum, much too hard and fast to be her own heart. She knew *its* beat! But it had to be her heart, because it pounded so hard she could hardly breathe. She felt fluttery all over. She had never felt the least bit like this before.

"If I can," she whispered through the beating.

Black Wolf set down the bucket. He opened his bright-striped blanket, and drew Annie into it, and folded it around them both. They stood there outside the tipi, looking at each other, and Black Wolf brought up his hand from around Annie's waist and stroked her hair.

"Such funny hair," he whispered. "Like sumach leaves in the fall."

"Oh," Annie said, and pushed against him. "You'd better let me go. If people see us standing here like this, they'll think we're courting."

"Aren't we?" asked Black Wolf.

"Come in," Maa said, from the tipi door behind them, and they turned with a jump.

Maa picked up the bucket and carried it into the tipi. She put it in its usual place. Then she jerked her chin at the back of the tipi, where Sahnko and William sat, in the men's place.

"Sit down," Maa invited Black Wolf.

Black Wolf sat down with the other two men, and Annie and Maa started to get supper. Nobody talked about anything in particular. All three men mentioned the weather. Sahnko told a long, winding story about a buffalo hunt he had gone on ten years ago, and Black Wolf listened and agreed as politely as if he had been there and remembered all about it.

Once or twice Maa asked if anyone wanted anything more to eat. Black Wolf always wanted more. He acted as if he had never eaten such good food in his life—or as if he had never eaten any food, and had to get filled up.

Maa served him without speaking to him or looking at him, as if he were already her son-in-law.

While Maa and Annie ate their own meal, Sahnko and Black Wolf passed the pipe back and forth between them, solemnly smoking. William never smoked, and the Kiowas had come to accept the fact, and not be hurt when he refused the pipe. On ceremonial occasions he laid his hand on the pipe as a proof of his agreement and good will, but he would not raise the stem to his lips.

"Where have you been?" Sahnko asked Black Wolf when the pipe was finished.

"To the fort."

"Did you see the buffalo soldiers?"

"Yes. They were just coming in. Big men, most of them, and big horses. Nah! About the only time we get to see good horses anymore is when we go and look at the soldiers!"

"That's true."

"They are very busy there. They are hiring lots of men as guides, scouts, woodcutters. Even some Caddos and Wichitas to go out and cut hay. I asked for a job as a guide. I hope I get it."

Sahnko's brow clouded over. "Why a guide?" he demanded. Annie hoped he wouldn't start talking about spies, the way he had the other night. But William must have soothed him down, for his next question was, "Why not get a job as an interpreter?"

"I don't speak good enough English. They might

laugh at me if I tried to interpret. I might make mistakes."

"You speak good Kiowa," Sahnko reminded him. "Nobody here would laugh at you."

"That isn't enough. I'd have to learn to speak good English."

"The interpreter is an important man; he is the bridge between the white men and yourselves. Why not find someone to teach you English?" William suggested.

Black Wolf's face brightened, and clouded over. "Where?" he queried. "I'm willing to work hard, and learn the best I can, but who's going to teach me?"

"Annie could," William observed.

"I guess she could," said the young man. He smiled, suddenly. "You know, I'm so used to thinking of her as a Kiowa, I forget sometimes she isn't. I forget she speaks English." He looked at Sahnko. "I'd like to learn from her," Black Wolf said. He started scratching patterns with his fingertip on the earth of the floor.

"I don't know that I want her to teach you," Sahnko observed. "Even if you want to learn, I don't know that I want her to teach you. It doesn't look nice, a young man and woman talking together all the time."

"People might say things," Maa added.

Annie sat as still as a field mouse with a horse galloping toward it. She wanted to burst out, to say all sorts of things, but Maa had trained her well, and she kept quiet. At times like this, the older people were supposed to speak, not the young women.

Probably, she thought, Sahnko and Maa knew what was going on. They had let her go to the spring, and meet Black Wolf there. They already knew what they would say when the time came for Black Wolf to speak to them. Annie knew that whatever answer Sahnko and Maa gave, she and Black Wolf would have to abide by it.

"Perhaps if he came here, and they sat and talked in the tipi, with Haynday Mah, people wouldn't say bad things," William suggested.

"Perhaps," Sahnko agreed. He refilled his pipe, and glanced toward Annie. "What do you say, Daughter? This is your life, too. You have to make your own decision."

Annie considered. Whatever decision she made now would be for the rest of her life, she knew that. "Yes," she almost whispered.

"Be sure," Maa cautioned her. "Do you really want to teach this young man English? It will be winter soon, and you will be indoors with me. At least this will fill in the time, if you are bored. What do you want to do?"

Annie sat and looked at the hem of her cloth dress. The thought flicked through her mind that the hardest thing she had ever tried to do was to teach Maa how to put a hem in a piece of fabric. She jerked her mind back where it was supposed to be; the other thought was silly.

Annie lifted her head. "I'll teach him, the best I can," she promised.

"When I have learned, and get a job at Fort Sill, then I can think about getting married," Black Wolf added. They looked across the tipi at each other, and there was nobody else there at all.

Two days later, before William left, he called Annie to help him bring the mules in from the pasture and hitch them to the wagon.

"Does thee love him, child?" he asked her, as they walked side-by-side over the dry grass.

"I—I don't know," Annie stammered. Love? That was something in Sir Walter Scott's novels, or the poems of Mr. Longfellow. Mother used to read them aloud to her sometimes. Love? Love didn't happen to ordinary people—or did it?

"Remember, child, thee are of different blood. It may make a difference in thy feelings, later on."

"How can it? What do you mean?"

"If he learns English, and becomes an interpreter at Fort Sill, thee must live there, among the white people. They will take thee into their homes readily, for thee is of their blood and coloring. How will they feel about thy Indian husband, though?"

"What if he is an Indian? He's as good as any of them! Better! Smarter, too. He *wants* to learn English. Do any of *them* want to learn Kiowa? Do they even try? Thee knows they do not."

"Annie, Annie, Annie." William laughed. "Is this the same girl I talked to last week? Is this the girl who argued with me that one man could steal himself from another?"

"That was different! We were talking about something else, then."

"Were we, Annie?" William asked, so quietly that Annie stopped walking, in order to hear him better. "Were we? I thought we talked then, as we do now, about what makes a man, and about what makes me. Isn't this the same?"

Annie thought for a long time, turning William's question over in the deepest part of her mind. At last she answered.

"I guess it is," she said. "I don't know, but I guess it is. It's hard." She twisted her hands together. "A year ago it would have been harder. There is something I haven't told thee."

"What is that, Annie?"

"A year ago, when we were at Fort Sill, I talked to a man there. He came through with a trail herd of cattle. He's a Choctaw."

"Yes?"

"We stopped at his place when I was a little girl, on the way west. He and his wife were the first Indians I ever saw. They were good to us."

"What did he tell thee?"

"He saw my folks. They stopped at his place again on

their way back from Texas. They were going to the Cherokee Nation.''

"Did he know where they were going? The Cherokee Nation is a big place, child.''

"No, he didn't know where. He said he would look for them and tell them where I was, but it might take him a long time to find them. He said for me to wait for word, and not to get worried or scared.''

"And would thee want thy parents to find thee married to an Indian? Remember, they must have thought thee dead this long time. Perhaps they have hated the Indians for taking thee—hated them the way thee used to say thee hated the Yankees.''

Annie hung her head. "Perhaps they do. Father always called them red devils and taught us to be afraid of them.''

"Now thee sees that they are not devils, but men, and thee has become as one of them since thee gained that understanding. To know people and to understand them is to like them and learn to live with them. Thee has discovered that for thyself, and thee may have to teach it to thy parents.''

"Not to Mother. I know I won't have to teach it to her. I expect Father will have to learn—perhaps from thee.''

"I will help thee all I can. Tell me, Annie, why did thee not tell me about this Choctaw man and his search for thy family before? I would have thought thee would have cried such glad news aloud to the treetops.''

"Because I was afraid . . . I thought that if I told thee I might make it not come true . . . talking about it might, I mean . . ."

"Annie, if thee believes that God will bring thy parents back to thee, talking about thy happiness and faith will not change the event. I wish thee had told me, so I could share thy joy with thee. Thee has told me now, however, and I can rejoice for thee."

"Does thee really think that they will hate Indians?"

"I hope not, for thy sake."

"What shall I do if they do hate him? Friend William, what shall I do?"

"Let thy heart tell thee when the time comes. Listen to the still, small voice of God, speaking in thy conscience, child. Now, tell me truly. Does thee love this young man? Can thee live with him always, and be a Kiowa, even if thy parents find thee?"

They stood under a bare elm tree. Its yellowed, acrid-smelling leaves heaped about their feet. The thin autumn sunlight, unsoftened by the tree's summer shadow, shone so brightly that no one could escape it. The light flooded Annie's mind and heart, as the sunlight washed over her body.

"I love him, Friend William," she said in a low voice. "I do love him. As for living like a Kiowa"—she lifted her head and looked him in the eye—"why, that's the only way that I know how to live." She stopped, and thought some more. "I don't know how or when we can get married," she resumed. "All the Indians have a hard time these days. There's no buffalo left to hunt, no deer —nothing. If we didn't have rations, we couldn't eat. If Maa couldn't make moccasins, we wouldn't have clothes, or be able to get canvas for a tipi. I don't know how we can live when we get married, but it won't be this way, anyhow. We can't live the old Kiowa life—it isn't here anymore."

"That is true. God has given thee the wisdom to see the changes that are coming about."

"God has given Black Wolf the same wisdom!"

"That is also true. He is still an Indian, though, Annie. He may see that changes are coming, and think he can adjust to them, but he cannot do it alone. Thy love must guide him along the new trail that is ahead of the Indians."

"I can try."

"Annie Donovan," William said, "never in all the years that I have known thee has thee given me thy outright promise. Never has thee said, 'I will,' but only, 'I will try.' It is time for a change. Unless thee can say 'I will,' thee had better not marry anybody."

"I will use my love to help him."

"Good, then. Thee will do that." They walked on. "And during the winter, thee can use thy love to teach thy friends to speak English, and to learn new ways. The four of you can study together. Thee can have a school."

"That would be fun!"

"That will be fun, but it will be doing good, too. Here are the mules. Let us go back."

Together, they returned to the tipi. Annie helped with the harness, and watched her friend drive away.

Chapter Eight

Old Friends Meet

They were going to Fort Sill for rations the next day anyway. Sahnko had a wagon now. The government men had picked out a few Indians in each band who were what they called "progressive," and given them each a wagon. Maa had traded two saddle horses for two that were broken to harness. Now, when they went for rations, they rode in the wagon, and brought their supplies home in it.

Annie drove the team. She couldn't remember when she had learned to handle a harness team; it was so long ago that she had forgotten. Before they went to Texas, she was sure. She still knew how to do it. Maa sat beside her, upright and correct, holding a red-and-blue-striped parasol above them both. Annie was glad of the parasol. Her fair skin still burned easily.

The brown autumn prairies spread all around them. Sahnko, in the back of the wagon, drummed with his fingers on the floor, and sang a soft little song. It was familiar, but Annie was slow to place it. Then she remembered. It was the song the men sang in the Sun Dance lodge the day Maa and Sahnko adopted her. She had not heard it since. That had been the last Sun Dance the Kiowas ever held.

Hearing the song now made Annie happy and sad. She was so close to Maa and Sahnko—they had been such dear and loving parents to her—that it was hard to believe she could leave them for her own home when she married. But she would, of course. Kiowa girls always set up their own households. And besides, Annie and Black Wolf would live at the fort, if they were interpreters.

They ate their noon lunch beside a spring where water cress grew thick. The cottonwoods had lost their leaves, and the drifted gold lay about them on the ground. Only the thin shadows of the branches fell across Annie's dress, but she didn't mind. The sunshine and the delicate shadows were all part of the day; a day that was sweet and sad and that she would always remember. She didn't know why.

Annie would search for the young woman with the Southern voice at the trading post. Sometimes she saw her, and the woman smiled at her. More often the woman was not there, and Annie and Maa did their trading alone and waited for Sahnko to come back with the rations in the wagon. Most of the women did that. Let the men go and deal with the soldiers, Maa sometimes said. The women made the moccasins and beaded bags and loom-woven bead necklaces the trader took, and they had the right to choose the things they wanted for their families.

Today Sahnko was late getting back with the wagon. He had half a beef piled in the back, along with the other things. "They issued extra stock today," he said to Maa. "A trail herd came through going to Dodge City, and dropped off more head than they had contracted for. Said the country was so dry, they couldn't trail them all through."

"Good," Maa replied. "We can dry it." She looked at the dropping sun. "The weather's cool enough. The meat will keep till we get home tomorrow. Let's camp here tonight and get an early start in the morning."

Lots of family groups were making camp in the grove beyond the red store. The stream from which they usually drew their water had gone dry, but the storekeeper was generous, and let them use his pump. Maa had never seen a dug well or a pump before, so Annie told her all about it, and showed her how the long iron handle worked.

The smell of wood smoke from the cooking fires hung over the camp, a perfumed smell, like the blue tinge the smoke gave the air. It was a funny thing. The smell grew stronger and it changed in character as they finished their meal. It was no longer a blue smell but a yellow one; not a perfume but a choking stench. The light around them had changed, too. There should have been the white moonlight of a clear autumn night, but the light growing in the northwest and sweeping toward them was yellow, tinged with red. From the northwest!

Everyone in the camp, it seemed, saw that ominous glow at the same time. Everyone moved at once. The women loaded the wagons, while the men hitched up the teams. The horses had smelled the smoke, and their fright was growing. They were pitching and unruly; some even bucked in the wagon shafts. Annie fought to hold their team until Maa and Sahnko finished loading, and Maa was safely on the seat beside her. Annie clung to the lines, waiting for Sahnko.

"Go on," he ordered from the ground. "Men will stay here. We'll save as much as we can."

"Don't stay!" Annie cried. "Father, don't!"

Sparks were falling all around them now. The horses were going crazy.

"I'll be all right," Sahnko reassured Maa and Annie. "Go on. Take your mother down to the railroad tracks. They keep the ground clear of brush and high grass there. We've done this before. See! The soldiers are there!" He gestured toward a line of silhouettes, black against the glow. The soldiers were out along the crest of the hill, racing toward the oncoming fire, beating the blaze down with what looked like tow sacks.

A man ran from the store with tin buckets strung along his arms, clanking like bracelets. "Come on," he yelled at Sahnko. "We can line up and pass the water from the well. Save the store, and we may save the camp!"

"Go on!" Sahnko ordered again. Annie shook the lines over the horses' backs and headed the team down for the open course of the railroad tracks. The fire had reached the crest of the hill behind them, and the soldiers were retreating before it.

The women huddled in their wagons along the tracks. Children whimpered and clung, although none of them cried aloud. This was probably the safest place they could have gone, and even so smoke and sparks reached them on the north wind. The fire must have started suddenly, perhaps from one dry twig rubbing against another. It had raced across the plains almost as soon as there was a spark. It was not as big a fire as the one Sahnko's father remembered, but it was big enough and destructive enough to frighten anyone who saw it.

Annie and Maa watched the flames rage toward the store and the camp; watched the blaze pile up as it seized the frame building. And then they watched the fire roll back, before a sudden strong south wind that swept it away from the struggling men.

"The owl," Maa said suddenly, softly. "The owl. He told us something bad would happen. This is what he meant, that old owl."

"It's going away!" Annie exclaimed. "Look, Maa, it's going away."

"Yes, it's going away," Maa echoed. "Where's your father? Why doesn't he come? Did the owl take him, too? Here come the buffalo soldiers, but no Indians. What are they going to do with us? What do they want? Will they chase us?"

Troopers were riding toward them, outlined against the last glow of the fire. A young man with a sergeant's stripes on his sleeves led the group. His dark features were lost in the darkness through which he rode. Then he turned his head to give an order, and Annie saw his profile against the dying firelight.

"Deut!" she screamed. "Deut!"

The young man jerked around in his saddle. His eyes ran over the bunched wagons, the nervous horses, and the clustering frightened women and children, searching for the source of her voice.

"Deut!" Annie cried out again. She had wanted to hide when she talked to Bill Jim, and keep her meeting with him secret from everybody. Now she wanted to run out. She didn't care who saw her; this was different. Deut was her home folks! She thrust the reins into Maa's hands, and jumped down from the wagon seat. "Deut!" Annie cried, running forward. "Don't you know me, Deut?" She held out her arms "I'm Annie!"

The sergeant had already drawn rein. Now he was out of the saddle in one movement. He ran toward the girl who was running to meet him. Then they had their arms around each other, as if they were brother and sister, crying and laughing and talking at once. Maa and the other women in the wagons sat and stared. The troopers drew up and waited.

"Are you all right?" Deut and Annie said at the same time, and laughed again, and waited.

"You say," Deut said. "Ladies first," he reminded Annie.

"I'm all right. Are you?"

"Yes, yes, I'm all right. Fire's out and nobody's hurt. Were you in the camp?"

"Yes. I guess everything we had is gone."

"Nobody can stay in that camp tonight. We got orders to bring all you—ladies—up to the parade ground and have you stay there till morning." He hesitated. "They'll get some blankets and make a kind of camp."

"That's all right. We'll get along."

"I can't let you sleep out that way, Miss Annie! I'm going to take you to my captain's wife. She comes from Georgia. She'll understand about a lady. She'll look after you.

"I have my mother—my Kiowa mother—"

Deut pondered momentarily. "You bring her, too. Mrs. Scott won't mind, I'm sure. Go up to the parade ground and wait with the others. I'll come and fetch you."

The troops escorted the straggle of wagons back up the hill and onto the parade ground. Men were bringing blankets from the quartermaster's stores building on the south side of the square, and piling them at the foot of the flagpole in the center. Others were issuing the blankets to Indians as the Kiowas came forward to get them. The moon had risen and its white light fought with the last red-and-yellow fire glow, so that at one time people's faces and bodies looked one color, and then another.

Annie and Maa waited and watched for Sahnko near the stores building. They asked anyone who would stop and speak to them about him, but no one seemed to have seen him since the bucket brigade formed.

Maa did not cry, but she whispered, "That owl. That owl," over and over, until Annie thought she would scream like an owl herself.

Deut found them when the excitement had subsided a little. He was on foot now, and he first led the weary team to a picket line where other Kiowa wagons were parked and horses were tied. Then he guided Annie and Maa to a house set back from the parade ground, in the second row of buildings on the north side of the fort.

It was all part of the strangeness and the sadness and the wonder of that night that the captain's wife turned out to be the young woman Annie had watched in the trading post. Her little boy still hung back when Deut led Annie and Maa into the kitchen, but the mother came forward with her hand outstretched.

"This is Miss Annie Donovan, Mrs. Scott," Deut introduced them. Annie remembered how particular Sadie had always been about manners. "She's my folks. My daddy and mammy worked for hers before I was born. They belonged to them, before the war. This Indian lady she says is her Kiowa mother." He sounded a little uncertain about the last.

"How do you do, Annie Donovan? I'm Letitia Scott,

and I'm mighty glad to meet you. How did you get with the Indians, if it isn't a rude question?"

"I was captured when I was ten. This is my Kiowa mother, Mrs. Scott. You call her Haynday Mah."

"How do you do?" Mrs. Scott said, extending her hand. After a moment Maa laid her own palm against the white one.

"I'm glad to have you both," Mrs. Scott went on. "You will have to forgive Captain Scott. He's out with the men, getting things settled down, or I'm sure he'd be here to meet you."

"That's all right," Annie murmured. This woman was mighty formal, she thought. A Georgian—that explained it. But she was a Georgian married to a Yankee officer! How could anyone explain that?

"Come on," Mrs. Scott encouraged her. "You look half dead. I know you want to clean up. My maid has the guest room ready for you. We can get acquainted in the morning." She glanced at Deut. "That's all we need, thank you, Sergeant Donovan. With Captain Scott's permission you can come and talk to Miss Donovan in the morning. You must have a lot to say to each other."

"Thank you, ma'am," Deut assented. He closed the kitchen door quietly behind him.

Mrs. Scott's guest room was as pretty a place as Annie had ever seen. The walls were papered in blue-and-white stripes with field flowers printed over them. Mrs. Scott had hung pictures around the room. There was one of

[142]

cows in a meadow, up to their shoulders in green grass, that made Annie homesick for Tennessee as she had not been for years.

There was a flounced dressing table with a gold-framed mirror hung above it. There was a marble-topped com- mode stand, with a flowered china basin and pitcher standing on it. There were clean towels on the rack beside the stand, and clean sheets on the bed the maid had turned down for them.

"Have you everything you need?" Letitia Scott asked.

"Yes, thank you," Annie replied. She paused for a moment. "It is very kind of thee to take us in this way," she said, trying to be formal herself. "We are grateful."

"Oh, dear, that's all right, don't think a thing of it, we're glad to have you," Letitia Scott replied. "Get a good rest now. Good night." She closed the door behind her.

Maa looked at Annie, and then down at her own dress, and shook her head. Annie looked in the mirror, and saw them reflected there, standing side by side. They were both streaked with dust and soot. There were little spark holes burned in their dresses and moccasins. Their hair was tousled and dusty.

"I hope Father's all right," Maa fretted. "I'd like to know he has a place to sleep and somebody to get break- fast for him."

Annie felt the same way, but she trusted Deut's word that nobody in the bucket brigade at the store had been hurt.

"We'll find him in the morning," she encouraged Maa. "Let's clean up and go to bed, so we can look for him if we have to."

"We need to wash," Maa agreed. "I am tired, and so are you."

"Here you are," Annie announced. She poured water from the pitcher into the bowl, and handed Maa the brown, transparent cake of Pear's soap from the painted-china soap dish.

"All that water?" Maa asked. "What will you do?"

"You use it," Annie said. She glanced down into the pitcher. "There's plenty left. Go on, use that." A tap at the door interrupted her.

Mrs. Scott stood outside, with lacy-trimmed whiteness across her arm. "I forgot," she said apologetically. "I hope I didn't disturb you."

"No, you didn't," Annie replied.

"I remembered everything you had was probably burned up. Here are nightgowns for you. Good night again."

"Thank you," answered Annie dazedly.

She sat on the floor, at the edge of the rug, and looked around her while Maa washed. A painted-china washstand set! Pear's soap, which Mother used to keep in her trunk and allowed Annie to wash with only before services on Sundays! Wallpaper! A turned-down bed, with sheets! And now white percale nightgowns with lace and insertion trimmings! Annie Donovan—Indian Annie

Donovan—had forgotten that many of these things ever existed.

Neither Maa nor Annie slept well that night. Even with the windows propped open, the room seemed close and its air dense. The bed was so soft it smothered them, and the sheets felt slippery with ironing.

After an hour or so of trying to breathe on a feather pillow, Maa got up. She took a blanket that was folded on the foot of the bed, and stretched out on it on the floor. At least Maa would rest there, Annie decided, even if she couldn't sleep.

Whenever Annie herself closed her eyes, pictures formed before them. The wall of fire came sweeping toward her. The horses bucked in the shafts, and she fought them down. Her arms still ached. Against the rolling wave of flames she saw Deut again, over and over. He turned his head and his profile against the light was just like his father's, sharp and chiseled like the pictures of Arabs in *Harper's Monthly Magazine.*

People said that all Negroes looked alike, but that wasn't so and Annie knew it. All that statement meant was that the people who said so hadn't seen many Negroes. The same people would probably say all Indians looked alike! They'd say Annie shouldn't shake hands with a Negro, let alone hug him. Deut was like her brother. They were brought up together until Annie went away. She'd hug Bud if she saw him, wouldn't she?

Maa sighed, and her voice came softly from the floor.

"Will you go back?"

"Back? Back where? To camp?" Annie questioned drowsily. "I don't understand."

"I think you do," Maa said, sadly. "This man tonight. This buffalo soldier. He knows where your own mother is, doesn't he? He can take you to her? Don't you want to go back there—with them?"

Without even thinking, Annie slid off the bed and down onto the floor beside Maa. She took the older woman in her arms and held her tight, as Maa used to hold her, when she first came to the Kiowa camp. "Do you want me to go away?" Annie asked.

"Go away? You? The daughter that I raised to be a woman? My heart would go out of my body if you left me. I think I would die," Maa answered slowly.

"Then I'm going to stay! That's all there is to it."

"Think about that," Maa warned her. "Think about that a long time. Maybe by morning you will want to go. If you go you can have all these—these—things"— she gestured at the unnamed objects clustered around her in the room—"and you know what they are, and what to do with them. Maybe you would be happier if you went." Her voice broke. "I won't keep you from being happy."

"I could have these things here, if I wanted them," Annie declared. "If Black Wolf works hard and I help him we can earn enough money to buy them, if we want to. I don't see why we'd need them, but if you want them we'll earn enough to get them for you. Right now, I'd rather earn the money for a good secondhand tent and a cookstove, until we have time to stitch up a tipi. We've got to have a place to live."

Maa abandoned the lures of material possessions. "Don't you want to see your own parents? Your brothers and sister?" she inquired.

Her words startled Annie, and sent a new thought racing through her brain. If she saw her own parents, and her brothers and sister, would she know them? Would they know her, if it came to that? She had recognized Deut, but he hadn't recognized her. Was she so changed and different from the ten-year-old Annie Donovan, this Indian Annie, that nobody in her other world would know her, and she would only dimly know them? It was too deep a question to answer.

She clung to Maa. "I wouldn't know them! I don't know them! I hardly even remember them! It's all so long ago to me. I used to miss them terribly, but now I have you and Father, and I don't feel the same way. I'd be afraid to see them now."

Maa patted her back and stroked her hair, still rough and dirty from the fire, although Annie had used the hairbrush on the dressing table and tried to straighten and smooth it. "Don't cry, Daughter. Wait until morning, until you can talk to that black white man. He can tell you what you need to know, I think."

Gradually Annie calmed down. "May I lie down here,

on the blanket, beside you? It's coming daylight anyway."

"Yes," Maa said. She moved over to make room for Annie on the blanket. Somewhere a rooster crowed, as they drifted off to sleep.

Chapter Nine

The Decision

The house was quiet when Annie woke up. There was a smell of coffee and bacon in the air, a tempting, promising, comforting smell. Annie realized that she was hungry.

Maa sat on the floor, with her back against the wall, washed, and with her hair brushed and braided. "I couldn't find Sahnko," she said. "I went out to look for him as soon as the sun was up. Several people said they saw him last night, and he was all right. I told them where we were."

"He'll find us," Annie consoled her. She got up and folded the blanket before she washed, and again tried to brush the tangles out of her hair. She had no elm-twig toothbrush, and had to be satisfied with rinsing her mouth out with water. There was a knock on the door.

When Annie opened the door, she found the little boy standing just outside it. He looked shy, and a little scared, but he was there.

"Good morning," Annie said. She held out her hand, and after a moment he gravely shook it. "What's your name?" Annie asked him.

"Walter Ivanhoe Scott," he answered. "Is yours Annie Donovan?"

"Yes, it is."

"Mother says come to breakfast," said Walter Ivanhoe, and led the way downstairs.

Annie and Maa followed him into a sunny dining room. The round table in its center was set with blue-and-white china, and there was a glass vase of flowers in the middle. There were silver spoons, and knives and forks. Annie had never seen silver tableware except Mrs. Cantrell's, and she certainly had never expected to eat from it again. She sat down in the place Letitia Scott pointed out to her, and Maa sat down beside her, with her legs hanging off the chair. Captain Scott came in as they were getting settled, and took his place at the head of the table.

"Good morning, Miss Donovan," he said, and then, in the same tone, he went on, "Will you ask the blessing?"

Annie was startled almost to death. That was part of a man's duty, not a woman's! Then she noticed that the Scotts were all looking at her and waiting for her, and she bowed her head.

"For this and every blessing we receive at Thy bountiful hand," Annie repeated William George's Grace, "O Lord, make us truly thankful. For Jesus' sake. Amen."

There was a little pause after she finished, and then a Negro maid brought in platters of scrambled eggs and crisp, thin-sliced bacon, and set them, with the serving plates, before Captain Scott. The girl passed the plates as he served them, and then went around the table with hominy grits and butter and gravy, fluffy light hot biscuits, and strawberry jam.

Annie saw Maa's eyes opening wider and wider as she looked at the strange foods. But Maa was brave. She let the maid help her, as she served everybody else. Each time a new food went on her plate, Maa waited a fraction of a second before she began to eat. She watched to see what Annie would do with the tableware. Neither of them spoke a word about the strange utensils. They did not even talk about the big square white-linen table napkins. Annie unfolded hers, so did Maa.

Indeed, nobody said much of anything until breakfast ended. Then Captain Scott turned to Annie. "Sergeant Donovan tells me that he knew you and your family before you were captured."

Sergeant Donovan! Deut! Well, of course. Slaves always took their masters' names, and he and his family must have kept the Donovans'.

"That's right," Annie said steadily. "His folks have worked for mine since before we were born."

"Do you want to tell me about your captivity? We will have to make an official report of your rescue, you know. Were you mistreated? Were you hungry, or beaten?"

"What makes you ask that?"

"For the report, for one thing. For another, if you did suffer, then we can pick up the people who injured you, and punish them. We have standing orders to return all prisoners to their families, and to make sure they are in good health, and have not been abused."

"Nobody ought to be punished on my account," Annie replied. "You can report that I had the best treatment anybody could give me. I was their adopted daughter, and they treated me like a real one. Oh, I went hungry sometimes. Everybody else did, too. That was after the white hunters killed off the buffalo, and before the Army began to give us rations. Thee has heard about that time? It was hard for all the Indians."

"Yes, I know about it; I was stationed here then. It was necessary, Miss Donovan. Our orders were to protect the settlers coming into the country, at any cost."

"Did you ever think about protecting us?"

"Us? Who do you mean by us? I don't understand you."

"The Kiowas. All the Indians."

Annie's head was up and her temper was higher. This man—this stupid Yankee—had been one of those who starved the Kiowas; probably one of the troops who held the people captive in the horse corral. And he talked about protecting the settlers! She knew how Mother had felt when she told the trooper to go back to Indiana. She wished this man would go back to his home, wherever it was.

"Where did thee come from, to come here?" she asked.

Almost absent-mindedly he answered her, "Springfield, Illinois."

"From Old Abe's town!"

"From Old Abe's town."

"You know what he stood for. The right of all people to be free and to belong to themselves. That's what we were told because we wanted to keep our slaves." Unconsciously, she quoted William. "If you don't think one man can own another, why do you think it's right for one man to starve another?"

The captain was silent a moment. He had picked up a fine silver spoon from the table, and now he held it, turning it over and over in his hand, as if he had forgotten what it was.

"That's a strange way for you to talk," Captain Scott said at length. "You talk as if you hated your own people, not the Indians."

"The Kiowas are my people," Annie said, and knew that her words were true, and would always be true.

"You must have some feeling for your own parents."

"I love them. I want to see them. I can't leave here to live with them, I'm afraid."

"Well, I've telegraphed to them to tell them where you are. Sergeant Donovan gave me their address in the Cherokee Nation. I should have an answer tomorrow, and know whether they are coming to get you, or will send you the fare to go to them."

[153]

"I can't go to them!"

"Then I suppose they'll have to try to come to you."

"I want to see them; I want to see all my family. I don't think I'll know them when I do see them, or that they'll know me. We'll all be strangers to one another, that's the trouble. Deut didn't recognize me, last night. And I can't go away with them."

"Well," Captain Scott said, kindly, "after all, we'll see how you feel when I get the answer to my telegram. If you want to, you can wait here, with my wife. If you'd like to keep this woman with you—your mother, you called her—that's all right, too. Mrs. Scott won't mind."

Annie's eyes rested on Maa's hands, twisted a little, and thickened from hard work; from making moccasins to trade for cloth for Annie's dresses, from caring for people in need. . . . Her eyes strayed to the narrow, pink-nailed fingers with which Letitia Scott was arranging and rearranging the flowers in the bowl on the table.

"I thank thee for thy kindness. I'll go back to camp with her."

"Why should you? You can stay here and be comfortable."

"She needs me. She has not found her husband since the fire. We need to look for him."

"But my wife will be glad to help you—lend you new clothes—do everything possible to keep you comfortable."

In spite of all the seriousness of that morning, Annie had to laugh. "I guess being comfortable is what thee is used to," she said. "I've forgotten how to live in a house and wear white-girl clothes. I'll be better off and more comfortable in camp."

"Will you give me your word to stay there and wait for your parents, or for word from them? Will you promise not to run away?"

A wave of desolation such as she had not felt since that first day in the canyon, when she realized that she was Sahnko's prisoner, swept over Annie Donovan. She *could* not run away. Where was there to run to? She, like all the other Kiowas, was a prisoner. They were prisoners of the strength this man represented. His railroad tracks and telegraph wires were the walls of their cage. His guns were the bars on its doors.

"I give thee my word I won't try to run away," Annie said solemnly. "I promise that I won't leave the camp. May Deut come to see me?"

"Sergeant Donovan?" Captain Scott said rather stiffly. "Yes, as soon as he is off duty. I'm sorry you can't see your way to accept our invitation. My wife would have enjoyed having you as her guest."

"Please stay," Letitia Scott begged in her soft voice. "I'd love to have both of you stay."

"Thanks to thee," Annie said, "but I think we'd better go back to the camp. My father—my Kiowa father—doesn't know where we are, and we haven't found him yet. We're both worried about him. The last we saw of him, he was in the bucket brigade at the store."

"I'm sure he's all right," said the Captain. "We have no reports of any injuries from there."

"What did they say?" Maa asked in Kiowa. "What are you all talking about?" Annie repeated the English conversation for her. Captain Scott listened intently.

"Can you interpret?" he asked when Annie had finished.

"Only English and Kiowa. I don't know any other Indian languages."

"I see. Have you ever thought of looking for work as an interpreter?"

"Oh, yes," Annie replied. "I want to have a school for some of my friends this winter, so they can learn English well enough to interpret, too. There are four of us—"

"Women make good interpreters," said Captain Scott, thoughtfully, "but it's hard to take them out with the troops. We need interpreters at the school, and the doctor needs them all the time. We need men, though. Could you teach a man?"

"Well," Annie said, uncertain whether to laugh or to blush, "I have two young men in my class."

"Oh!" exclaimed Letitia Scott.

"Yes!" said Annie.

"Well, that's a reason," Mrs. Scott assured her. "I don't know that I could marry an Indian myself—"

"Thee married a Yankee," Annie reminded her.

"Yes, I did. I went to visit a school friend in Virginia,

and he was stationed there. And I—we—just fell in love."

"Thee must have been taught to hate the Yankees when thee was a child. I was."

"When I knew him, I loved him." They were talking to each other as if they were alone in the world.

Maa spoke, fretfully and wearily.

"My mother says," Annie began, and this time she did not use the qualifying phrase, "my Kiowa mother," "that we must go now. She is very tired, and we must find my father. She thanks thee, as I do. She is glad she came here. She used to be afraid of the officers' wives when she saw them in the store. Their hair and skins were light and pink, and they wore pretty dresses. Now she sees that they can be kind and good, like other people. She is glad to have stayed here, because you have taught her white women can be kind."

"Oh," said Letitia Scott faintly.

Sahnko was there waiting for them when they reached the place that had been their camp.

"Where were you all night?" he demanded. "What happened to you? I looked for you everywhere, and all anybody knew was that one of the buffalo soldiers had taken you away. Why did he want to do that?"

"We'll tell you later," Maa said firmly. She had recovered from her tiredness and fright as soon as she saw

Sahnko. "Did you get any breakfast? Are you all right?"

"Oh, I'm all right," Sahnko said, as if nobody cared. "I didn't get hurt in the fire, and I found a place to sleep back of the store, near the pump, with some other men. And then Spear Girl's mother gave me breakfast. I'm all right. What happened to you?"

"You tell him," Maa instructed Annie.

"The buffalo soldier is a man whose parents used to work for mine," Annie said, slowly and clearly. "He knows where they are, and he is coming here later on to tell me about them. He took us to his captain, and we spent the night there. This morning they gave us food, and we came back here."

"Is he going to tell your parents where you are? Let's sit down somewhere. I'm tired," Sahnko said.

They brushed a spot of ground bare of ashes, and sat down. Annie was tired herself, as tired as Sahnko sounded.

"The captain sent them word on the singing wires this morning," she told him.

"Do you want to go back to them?" Sahnko asked.

Annie wanted to cry. She wanted to scream. She wanted to throw back her head and howl her throat out like a coyote, she was so tired of hearing that question.

"I want to see my folks, yes," she answered as calmly as she could manage. "I still love them, or I love what I remember of them. I'm afraid I won't recognize them when I meet them, and I know they won't recognize me. I don't know what we can talk to each other about."

"I guess that's so," Sahnko agreed thoughtfully.

"I want to stay here," Annie went on steadily. "This is the way I've learned to live. I don't know how to live their way any more. Last night, living in a house—it was bad. I couldn't breathe. I'd die if I had to live in one all the time."

"You stay here," Sahnko consoled her. And, in English, "Li'l girl. Ours."

Chapter Ten

Coming Together

It was strange how little Annie and Deut found to say to each other, at first. They sat that evening by the camp-fire, looking and looking at each other. Annie had thought they would start right in and talk for hours, but it was hard to get started. Maa made coffee and bread and put them down before them.

"Eat with us," Annie invited.

"Me? Eat with them Indians?" Deut demanded.

"Why not?" Annie returned. "I do. I have for years."

"I guess you had to," Deut replied, "but it's strange to think you'd eat with them, like they was folks."

Annie's mind flashed back to that dinner the night Father and Bud came home from the war. James had trapped the possum, and Sadie had cooked it. The two of them had waited on table while the Donovans ate, and Deut himself had pulled the rope that swished a willow branch over their heads and kept the flies off the food. Afterward, the black Donovan family ate their own meal in the kitchen. Never, never, even on the trip to Texas, had they all sat down to a meal together. She wondered if she should say any of this to Deut; should remind him that it was as strange for her to eat a meal with him as it was for him to eat one with the Indians. She decided not to.

"She fixed it for you, because you're my guest," she finally said. "You'll hurt her feelings if you don't eat a little."

"All right," Deut said, but he nibbled the bread and sipped the coffee as if the foods were strange to him, and he looked as if he were afraid he might find something dirty in his cup.

"It's all right," said Annie. "Don't, if you don't want to."

"Thank you, ma'am," Deut said, and he set down his cup with an air of relief.

"Tell me about my folks," Annie prompted.

"They're all fine now. Things were pretty bad for a while—after you got took. And then your father said it was no good sticking it out in Texas. He made us pack up, and we all went to the Cherokee Nation."

"I knew about that. A Choctaw man told me. You might remember him; we stopped at their place when we left home. He said you stopped there again, coming back."

"That's right; we did."

[161]

"He said he would look for my family, and get word to them where I was."

"I had a letter from Mr. Bud last month. He come through and told them you was alive, but all he knew, you was some place near Fort Sill. It's big country out here, Miss Annie. Mr. Bud, he asked me to look out for you or get word of you, so they could find you. Without that, they didn't know where to start looking."

"I didn't think of that. Just how big the Cherokee Nation is, and I didn't know where to look for them there."

"No, I guess you wouldn't, even if you could get there."

"Go on," Annie urged. "Tell me the rest."

"We went on north from that Choctaw's place. It's pretty country in through there, Miss Annie; pretty like back home. Hills, and little streams, and some swamps. It's hard traveling, though. We went on north, to a place called Tahlequah. It's the capital of the Cherokee Nation."

"Is it a town, or what?"

"It's a pretty big town, with brick buildings and a hotel and paved streets, a court house and a school . . . Oh, just everything a town has. Like a county seat."

"Did you all stay there?"

"Not for long. Your father found a Cherokee lawyer who didn't want to work his place himself, and was looking for a good tenant farmer. So your father leased the land from him—good, rich bottom land on the Illinois River—and he and my daddy went to work, clearing the land and working the place."

"How did they make out?"

"Miss Annie, you won't never in this world believe me. You know neither of them ever share cropped before— they'd have died first. But when they had it to do, they did it. They're better farmers than anybody around there, and was to begin with. And they got good land. They built that place up you might say out of nothing, that's what they did. All the Donovans can hold up their heads. They ain't no ornery cotton-pickin' share croppers. They're farmers."

"The Donovans always have had a right to hold their heads up. What about the others? Bud? And Danny? And Katherine?" She could not yet ask about her mother.

"They're all well. Mr. Bud's married—he went back to Virginia two years later and married that Cantrell girl he was stuck on—you remember. Her folks gave up the whole thing and went back to Virginia."

"Mary Sue Cantrell? Yes, I remember her. She was a nice girl, as I recollect."

"She's a real nice young lady, Miss Mary Sue. And they got two of the cutest little red-headed boys you ever saw, and there's another baby on the way that they're hoping will be a girl. Danny, he's just beginning to look at the girls, but Miss Katherine's been flirting around like a little bird for most of a year now. Your father says he don't know what come over her; she's just barely fifteen, and cutting her eyes at the boys all the time."

"Fifteen's pretty grown up. Lots of Indian girls get married when they're fifteen, and have families when they're sixteen. She's just acting normal."

"That's what your mother says—it's normal. She says he'd feel bad if Miss Katherine didn't have any beaus."

Annie laughed, and then sobered. "What about thee, Deut? And what about thy parents?"

"It's funny to hear you talk like that, Miss Annie. Captain Scott's maid—maybe you noticed her—she comes from Philadephia, and she talks that Quaker talk."

"I'll have to go back there sometimes and talk to her. The only person I've had to speak English with is a Quaker—William George. Are thee and this girl good friends, Deut?"

"You might say so, Miss Annie. We're fixin' to get married soon's my term's up. I think we'll go back to the Nation to live, when that time comes—work with the old folks."

"Has she ever lived on a farm?"

"No, ma'am, Miss Annie, Tabby never has. We figure she'll just have to learn."

Annie laughed again. "What about James and Sadie?"

"They're fine, Miss Annie, just fine." Deut paused a

moment. "Look, Miss Annie. Why don't you ask me about your own mother and father?"

Annie could not answer him at once. There was a whole stream of questions dammed up inside her, waiting to pour out when the floodgates opened, and she had to fight to find the words she needed to open the way. It was hard; there would be much to understand and explain on either side.

"Tell me, Deut," she said at last.

"First off, they're both all right. Miss Mary, she grieved for you for a long time after you—were taken. She never has given you up for dead. Captain Donovan said he didn't hope to find you living—or if you were you'd have been hurt so bad you'd better be dead."

"Oh, no!" Annie cried.

"Miss Mary always said she'd find you alive and whole, even if it was in Heaven."

"How is she?"

"Miss Annie, you won't know her when you see her. Her hair went gray right off, and she's got little—she's so thin with grieving. She looks like an old lady some-times."

"Is she still so sad? Does she suffer as much now?"

"Not now, she don't. Not any more. She broke her heart for you the first five years, and she never gave up, like I said. Then she had another little baby girl. She said God gave her that baby to comfort her, although she

[165]

knew the baby couldn't take your place. Miss Mary cheered up after that, though. Now she's like herself again, except for the way she looks."

"What's the baby's name?"

"Grace, because Miss Mary said she took heart of grace after she was born."

"It's a pretty name. Deut, has thee any idea when they can get here?"

"I don't rightly know, Miss Annie. Captain Scott said it would take a day for his telegram to reach them. Then two days on the cars to get here. And it might take them a while to get ready—maybe they'd have to wait on crops and not get here till later."

"It's fall. What crops would they have to wait on? Oh, I remember. The cotton. They'd be picking."

"That's the one thing makes me wonder 'bout goin' back to farmin'—cotton pickin'—I do so hate gettin' my hands cut up with them bolls!"

"Yes, but the crop brings good money."

"That it does. Well, Miss Annie, I just can't rightly say when we ought to start looking for them. But if the cap'n hears, I'll let you know, I promise. And you'll stay here, won't you?" A bugle cut across his words. "All in."

"I promised. Deut, please come and talk to me again. And bring your Tabby, won't you?"

"As soon as ever I can and whenever I can, Miss Annie."

"Good night, Deut."

"Good night, Miss Annie." He walked away, lost and drowned in the darkness.

The camp near the burned-out store was a dismal place. Maa and Sahnko stayed with Annie, and they all waited together for Annie's family to come. Annie wanted terribly to send a word to Black Wolf and Spear Girl where she was, and why she was staying, but there was no one to take the message. Not even William George, who surely, surely would have gone for Annie's friends.

She knew how word gets around in the Indian world, without messengers, but she had never gotten over being surprised by the quickness of its spread. Almost before she had time to think her wish, Maa called her to come and look. Annie crawled out of the improvised shelter of brush and small sticks where she had huddled unhappily, and looked to the north.

Three horses were coming toward them down the hill. The riders were two men and a woman. Annie looked and looked again; then one rider kneed his horse forward, ahead of the others, pressing toward them, downhill and over the uneven burned-off ground.

The horse did not trip, and the rider stayed on his back until they stopped before Annie, and a young man slid to the ground.

"I didn't know what had happened to you," Black Wolf said, opening his arms. "They told me a soldier took you away."

Annie walked into his embrace, and they stood together, pressed together, for a long time or a little time. She never knew. She didn't care that Maa and Riding Away and Spear Girl were looking at them. She didn't care about anything in the world but her own happiness, growing and spreading inside her.

"It was somebody I knew," she said when she could free herself. "His parents work for mine, and we were children together. It's all right. I came back in the morning, and Maa was with me the whole time."

"You're going to stay, aren't you?" Black Wolf demanded. "You're not going away again, are you?"

"No," said Annie softly. "I'm never going away again." She looked up at him. "My folks may come to see me," she said. "We think they will. Will you stay here with me till they come?"

"We'll all stay," Spear Girl assured her. "We can start our school for interpreters right here in this camp."

"Good!" Annie said. "Then we won't lose any time."

"We'll get married right away—" Black Wolf began, but Maa interrupted him.

"No," she decreed. "She's not going to get married until she knows whether her own mother's coming, and until her mother has a chance to meet you. It isn't fair."

"They're married." Black Wolf jerked his chin at his friends.

"Her mother was there and gave permission. Sahnko and I won't, not until her mother is here."

"What are we going to do? Who's going to cook for me?"

"If all you care about is filling your stomach, I won't let her marry you at all."

Black Wolf began to laugh. "Get it all said now," he cautioned Maa. "Once you're my mother-in-law you'll be forbidden to talk to me. Remember, it's rude even to look at your son-in-law, let alone scold him."

"Oh, I'll remember," Maa said grimly. "Just make sure you do, too. As long as you're going to stay around here, and so I can keep an eye on both of you, I'll do the cooking this time."

"I knew all along you would," Black Wolf remarked, his eyes dancing.

In some ways that week was the best time Annie ever remembered. The waiting was hard, it was true. But Deut and Tabby came every other day; Spear Woman and Riding Away were with them, and two days later William George and his mules toiled into camp. They all ran to meet him and unhitch the mules.

"They told me thee was all right," he said to Annie.

"I had to see for myself. What is this news, child, that thee has found thy own?"

"Almost," Annie answered. "I found the boy whose parents work for mine. His captain telegraphed my people where I am, and made me promise to stay here until he hears from them. It's been eight days, now, and no word. I guess they're too busy to come, or maybe they can't afford it. I don't know."

William George looked across the camp, to the place where Black Wolf and Riding Away were helping Sahnko plait reins to replace his old ones. The two young men were practising English words aloud with each other.

"Thy school has opened, I see," William George said.

"My school has opened, but there's more than that. Captain Scott sends for me every day to interpret for him. I get paid fifty cents an hour for my work."

"That's a great deal of money," the Friend said gravely. "What does thee do with it?"

"I'm saving it. I want a wall tent and a cookstove of my own when we get married."

"Good girl. Thee has a clear-thinking head on thy shoulders, Annie. I'm glad of that, and happy for thee. Thee will be able to balance whatever problems come to thee in life, as, indeed, thee has always done."

The Army ambulance came down the hill and across the blackened ground while they were talking. Annie looked at it with mild curiosity. Once or twice Letitia

Scott had come to camp to see her. This was probably another such visit.

In fact, Letitia Scott was the first person out of the ambulance. She handed the reins to the trooper escort, and flung herself down like a girl. Then came a man—elderly, with a trim little gray beard. He gave his hand to the last two passengers in the ambulance, a woman and a little girl. The group walked slowly toward the camp.

Annie's curiosity turned to certainty. "Mother!" she cried, and ran forward. She took the older woman, gray and stooped now, in her arms, and clung as if she would never let go. The others waited for them.

"Annie Donovan," said Mother at length, holding her off at arm's length, "Look at you!" She shook her head. "All sunburn, and your hair a mop of tangles. I should think you'd be ashamed to let anyone see you looking such a mess, as big as you are." Her voice faltered and broke. "Oh, Annie, Annie," she sobbed, "to find you again, after all this time!"

Father came over, and put his arms around both of them. "Nobody hurt you, Mrs. Scott says," he said as if it were a question.

"Nobody hurt me. Everybody has been good to me." Annie reached out her hand to Maa, and drew the Kiowa woman close. "This is my other mother. I call her Maa, but her name is Haynday Mah."

The two older women looked at each other strangely

for a moment. Then Maa took Annie's hand, and put it in Mother's.

"I won't keep you away from her," she said. Maa was crying, too.

But Mother was always quick. She held Annie's hand, but she placed the other one in Maa's. The three stood linked for a moment. It was all right. Annie had two families, and a loved place in each, she knew.

Later, Annie sat with her parents under the trees, and held little Grace in her arms. Grace was the first Donovan Annie had ever seen who wasn't a red head. The little girl's soft curls were like the bright gold pieces in the trader's safe.

"You'll come back with us, Annie," Father said. "We can arrange for you to visit here sometimes, if you want to, but we came here to take you home."

Annie shook her head. "No, Father. I thank thee, but I can't go away. I'll come and visit with thee, but I belong here now."

"Of course you can!" Father said, suddenly angry. "There's no question about it. Everyone you love and everyone who loves you is back at Tahlequah. You can't live anywhere else."

"Not everyone, Father."

"What do you mean by that, young lady?"

They sat glaring at each other, and Mother intervened.

"You know they love her here, Michael. They don't want to lose her, any more than we did."

"Mary, that's an absurd thing to say. Absurd! We're her parents. We owe her a duty and she owes us one, aside from the matter of affection. She can't love these people more than she does us."

"Do you, Annie?" Mother's voice shook as she asked the question. "Do you love them more than you do us?"

"Oh, no! I love them just as much, in a different way, but that isn't it. There's—there's somebody else, too."

"And now what do you mean?" Father asked stiffly.

Mother looked at Annie, and it was she who answered.

"Annie's found another person here to love," she told him. "Who is it, dear?"

"I'll go get him," Annie said.

Black Wolf was waiting for her behind the shelter. His face was creased with worry. It cleared a little when Annie held out her hand to him, and led him back to face her parents.

"His name means Black Wolf. He's learning English," she told them.

"He is a good young man," said William George's quiet voice behind her. Annie didn't know where he came from. His support was all she needed.

"He's an Indian!" Father stormed. "His people stole her away from her home. Do you mean to stand there and tell me she wants to marry him?"

[173]

"She wants to marry him, and I think she should."

"What right have you to an opinion about my daughter's marriage, sir?"

"Father!" Annie cried. "You can't speak to him like that! He's been the only one I had who was—was like you and Mother. I won't let you talk to him that way."

"I'm against marrying anyone but your own people, Annie. Think. If you have children they will be half-breeds. You can't tell how they'll turn out."

"You can't tell how any child will turn out till it's grown and turned," Mother interposed. "I look at it differently. Once I wouldn't have, but now I do. Annie's like a missionary—a missionary teacher here. Mrs. Scott told us in the ambulance—you remember, Michael—how much good Annie has done teaching people to cook and sew. You wouldn't keep her from the mission field, would you?"

"No. But I wouldn't let her marry a native. I'm not going to."

"Thee has little to say in the matter, friend," William George said. "They love each other. They are good young people, who have waited for thee to come, before they married. It would have been easy to run away and marry in secret, in the old tribal way, but they did not. Annie has been a patient and dutiful daughter."

"Thanks for small blessings," Father muttered.

"Annie has lived this way too long to be happy any other. She does not feel about these people as thee does.

Give thy consent, and wish her happiness, my friend. It is the best thing thee can do."

Father stood unspeaking. Mother answered. "She has our consent," she said.

"Not mine." Father shook his head in stubborn negation. "I need to know a lot of things I don't. You say this is a fine young man, and for all I know, that's true. But what can he *do*? What kind of work is he fit for? Can he feed her? How are they going to live?"

"Those are serious questions," William George agreed.

"All my life I've heard about lazy Indians," Father persisted. "I've heard how the women work as long as they can stand up, from sun to sun, while the men sit around and do nothing. Do you think I want that kind of life for my daughter?"

"No decent man would. Thee is right to ask. Let me tell thee, from what I have seen and known for myself, that it is not true that Indian men are lazy. Indian women work all day long, every day. So do the women of our world, friend. Housework is housework, whether it's done within four walls or in a tipi."

"True for you," Mother inserted.

"But I have seen with my own eyes how hard Indian men work when there is work for them to do. They hunt from before daylight until long after dark; they are the finest light cavalry the world has ever known, says General Crook, and they are experienced horse-breeders and trainers. None of these are the employments of lazy men."

[175]

"No," said Father, slowly. "None of those is an unskilled trade. If they can breed horses, why can't they breed cattle, though?"

"Given time, they can. Given time, I doubt not that they will. In the meantime, Black Wolf is an interpreter-scout here at the post. He is paid—in cash—the same wages as a sergeant. At the same time, both he and Annie are given their share of whatever the tribe receives, from any source. And Annie will be paid for her work as a teacher and an interpreter. They will have a house. They will do as well as any young couple starting out in life. Better than most."

"Michael," Mother said softly, "remember when we first married? I had my linens and my household goods, from my mother. Your father gave us land and a house. We had one bed, a table, a chair, and a stool. We worked. We worked hard for everything we had. If my father hadn't left us Jim and Sadie, I don't know how we'd have made out sometimes. We know what hardship is. Annie's life was hard when we came to Texas. She's never known what soft living could be. Think, Michael."

Black Wolf spoke suddenly, slowly, in his careful English. "Annie loves thee all. Why do you hurt her? Look, she is ready to cry."

Father looked at Annie again, for the first time in minutes. She was too torn to bear any more. She leaned against Mother's shoulder, sobbing.

"Your people took her from us. No matter how good a

life you promise her, why should I give her back to you?"

"You don't give, you share." Black Wolf turned to Annie, and broke into a flood of Kiowa. "Tell him, my heart. Tell him we will come to see them, and they can come to see you. Tell him again that I will build a house for you, and when we are not living and working here, you will still live like a lady. Tell him I will learn to breed cattle—wohaws aren't different from horses that way, and there is plenty of land for them to run on. Tell him . . ." he stopped as suddenly as he had started, when Annie held up her hand.

"Father," she said, "my—my husband in my heart— wants me to tell you many things. He will bring me to see you. You know now how you can come here to see us and how welcome you will always be. And each of us knows the other is alive and well, and that if one of us gets sick, we can get to each other and help each other."

"That is true," Father said slowly. "It's the difference between life and death, when you put it that way."

"She is right," Mother reiterated. "Annie knows her heart, and she is right."

"It *is* the difference between life and death," Annie insisted. "He will learn to raise and feed cattle, he says. We will never be apart in the same way again. We will know each other to be alive. And he promises me—and you"—Annie giggled a little—"that he will build me a house, so I can always live like a lady even when I am not here at Fort Sill. Father"—she felt her voice fall apart—"he wants so much for thee to like him. He likes thee. Father, please believe that he is a good man."

Father looked again at Black Wolf, really looked at him, for the first time.

"We thought she was dead," he said slowly.

"She thought thee was," Black Wolf answered.

"How could she do other than she did?" William George queried. "She was not mistreated; she had the best that could be given her, but more than that she had love and care. She thought that all her family was lost to her. Now thee are all together again. Why not add to her happiness, and to thy own, by making thy family larger by another son?"

"Michael," Mother began, but Father shook his head. He threw up his hands in surrender.

"You are all right, and I know it," he said. "I want all my family together all the time. But they grow up; they marry and go away. Families scatter more now than they used to." He turned to Annie. "Will you write to us, regularly? Can you still write?"

"I can still write—and read letters if you write them," Annie said. Her heart was singing.

"Then we'll stay for the wedding and I'll give you away. It can be a real wedding, in the post chapel, can't it?" He asked William George.

"Certainly. There is no question."

"Father!" Annie cried. "I can't thank you. There isn't any way to thank you. But I love you and Mother more

[178]

than ever, if I can. And I'm so happy we'll all be one family again—"

Father put his arm around her, and laid the other arm on Black Wolf's shoulders. "Be good to each other, and be happy," he said. "We will see one another often."